A Time Away from Time

Michael Banister

Andrew Benzie Books
Martinez, California

Published by Andrew Benzie Books
www.andrewbenziebooks.com

Printed in the United States of America.

First Edition: January 2023

10 9 8 7 6 5 4 3 2 1

ISBN 978-1-950562-47-3

Cover and book design by Andrew Benzie

*A dream of the world as it could have been...
and will become.*

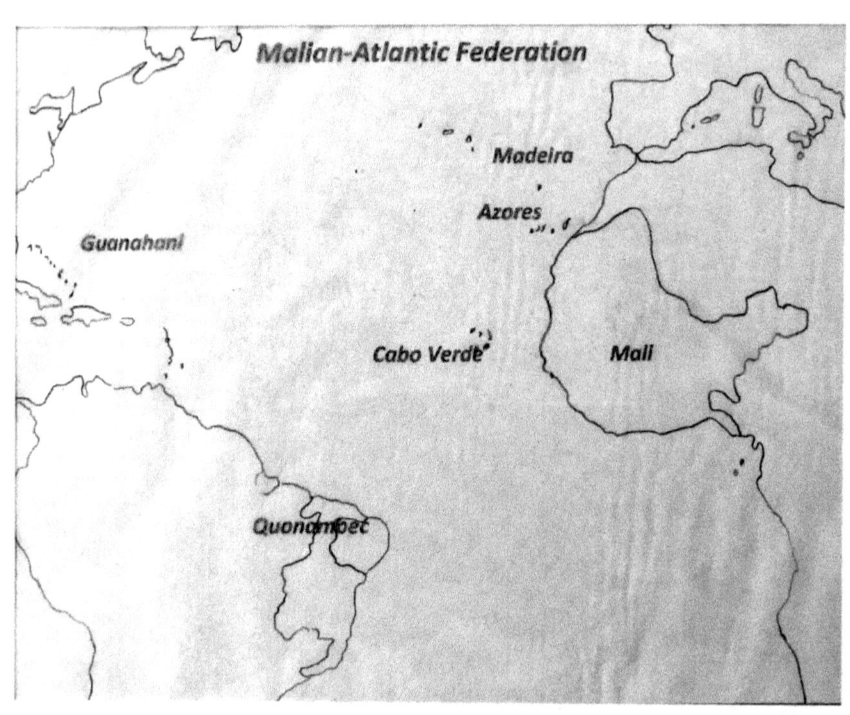

Malian-Atlantic Federation
Madeira
Azores
Guanahani
Cabo Verde
Mali
Quonampec

CHAPTER ONE

The year 1500

Father Martim Rodrigo sat in his study in the Church of Santa Clara in Oporto, Portugal, very worried about what he had found on his return to his beloved home. He was 70 years old, recently retired as priest of the small Catholic congregation in Mogadishu, Somalia, from 1460 to 1499. He had loved that congregation and that city. But he was ready to return to Portugal when the opportunity arose for him to take the position of chaplain aboard Vasco da Gama's fleet from 1499 to 1500.

Da Gama had been on the return voyage to Portugal from a successful trading trip around the southern end of Africa, up the east coast, and across the Indian Ocean to India. Da Gama had made that less-perilous outbound rounding of Africa without the benefit of the most advanced maritime navigation tool, the spherical astrolabe. Now, he faced a much more perilous journey back to Portugal.

But as his fleet dropped anchor off the bay of Mogadishu, east Africa, he was presented with a miraculous opportunity. The priest of the local congregation there offered da Gama a gift — a spherical astrolabe. Da Gama had been unable to obtain one before leaving Portugal. His fleet managed to round the Cape of Good Hope without disaster, but the return would be much more dangerous without better navigation. Not only did the priest, Father Martim

Rodrigo, offer da Gama the astrolabe, but he offered himself as chaplain to the expedition for the voyage back to Portugal.

Da Gama was very grateful to have Father Rodrigo aboard because it gave the sailors confidence that their voyage home would be under the shelter of Providence. As for da Gama, his confidence was bolstered more by the astrolabe than by having a priest aboard.

But although Rodrigo had hoped to have a most pleasant and hopeful voyage home, it didn't turn out that way. Far from it! When he first boarded da Gama's ship São Gabriel, he hadn't been aware of how sick the crew was. Many of them were dying. After a week, when the fleet arrived in Malindi, further down the coast of east Africa, half the crew had died, most during the crossing from India. Many of the rest were sick with scurvy. Since da Gama no longer had enough crewmen to sail three ships, he decided to transfer the freight from the São Rafael and scuttle the ship. The priest worked as hard as the rest of the crew, but it was difficult and exhausting work, especially in the hot tropical sun of that erstwhile paradise.

After the remaining two ships resumed the voyage, they managed to round the Cape of Good Hope thanks to the spherical astrolabe that one of Father Rodrigo's parishioners had given him. That leg of the voyage took approximately two months. When the two ships reached Santiago Island in the Cabo Verdes off the coast of west Africa, the captain of one of the two remaining ships, the Berrio, took the ship and continued on to Portugal.

Da Gama's brother Paulo had fallen seriously ill during the voyage up the coast of west Africa, so da Gama and Father Rodrigo elected to remain on Santiago Island in the hope of nursing Paulo back to health. Da Gama handed over command of his last ship, the São Rafael, to his clerk, who sailed the ship to Portugal. Da Gama, Paulo and the priest stayed a little longer on Santiago, but Paulo's health did not improve. They decided to take passage on a caravel back to Portugal, but Paulo died along the way. In gratitude to Father

Rodrigo for the use of the spherical astrolabe, da Gama returned it to the priest upon their arrival in Portugal.

But then when Father Rodrigo arrived home he was confronted by shock, followed by confusion, and then outrage. Slavery! Slaves working for the Church! This cannot be, he thought back to when he had his first meeting with Duke Àlvares. The duke, no doubt feeling generous, offered to "loan" to the Church three of his slaves. "They are sisters, 27-year-old Maryam, 30-year-old Sofia and 32-year-old Khadijah. They are strong and good workers. I purchased them at a slave auction on the Gambia River five years ago. I have been surprised at how quickly they learned our blessed Portuguese language! They were living in a town called Jenne and spoke only Arabic and a heathen language called Fulani."

Father Rodrigo still felt a sense of shock and anger when he thought back to that day. After the duke had left, Rodrigo chatted with the sisters for several minutes before he decided to ask the sisters about how they came to be brought to Oporto. He thought the sisters would be reluctant at first to talk about that. So he started out by saying, "I have agreed to have you work for the Church because I feel you otherwise might have a more difficult time working for the duke. Let me assure you I am utterly opposed to slavery."

That seemed to relax the women. Sofia spoke first. "Father, would you like us to tell you something about our experience?"

"Yes, if it wouldn't upset you. I don't know what the duke has told you about me, but I lived and worked for many years in a distant country in east Africa, where there was no slavery. Everyone was free. It was only after I arrived here, to the land where I was born, that I discovered that slavery has become commonplace. So, please, tell me your story."

Khadijah took a deep breath and began. "Our family was fairly well off in the town of Jenne, a very ancient town alongside the Bani River in central Mali. We owned a warehouse where we stored a great variety of goods brought into the town from the coast. My sisters and I managed the warehouse; we each had different responsibilities given to us by our parents who were at that time very elderly."

Khadijah stopped talking and wiped her eyes. She looked at her sister Maryam and asked her to continue.

Maryam sat silent for a few moments before she began. "My sisters and I had just finished the inventory of our parents' dry-goods warehouse in Jenne when it happened. First, there were the sounds of screams outside. When we ran outside to find out what was happening, we saw what looked like a dozen men attacking people and dragging them to two boats tied up at the shore of the river.

"Several men saw us and shouted to the others. Khadijah was the first to realize what was happening. She shouted, 'They're slavers! And they're dragging people to the boats. Inside, quickly!'"

"But we weren't fast enough. Although we made it inside, we hadn't managed to bar the door before it was pushed open by a large man who looked to be an Arab from the coast. He burst in, followed by several other men, and we were quickly grabbed and thrown to the floor."

Sofia placed her hand on Khadijah's and said, "Let me take over; you get yourself calm." Turning to Father Rodrigo she continued the story. "Our memory of the next few hours is hazy at best. I recall being beaten, bound and dragged outside to the boats. My sisters may have been beaten unconscious, or they fainted. As we were thrown into a boat, I saw a horrible sight. It seemed like at least ten more people were being abducted and forced into the boats.

"But then my memory was interrupted. I remember being hit; the blow probably knocked me unconscious. When I awoke, we were being carried off the boat. Some men tossed us into a horse-drawn cart full of similarly bound women and men."

Rodrigo motioned for Sofia to pause and then stood. "Let me bring you something to drink and eat. We can continue when you feel up to it."

Rodrigo brought the women tea, nuts and cheese. He could tell they were self-conscious at being asked to recount a very traumatic experience.

Once they had finished their tea, Khadijah resumed the story. "We were led to a large building on the coast of Mali. There were several large ships tied up at docks. The building had many cots, and there was a kitchen and tables set up outside. Men told us to go inside, sit on the cots and wait for meal time. They spoke Arabic to us, but I heard other men speaking your language. We did not know the Portuguese language at the time.

"They fed us and we slept. And the next day, the same. I think it was the day after that when we were taken to a large open field. Portuguese men from the ships bargained with the Arabs, and soon we were sold. That very afternoon we were taken on board a very large ship.

"We had never been on such a vessel, or taken a voyage of that length on the Great Ocean. Many weeks passed. We were sick. The food was terrible, rotten, and almost inedible.

"I'll spare you the rest of the story. We arrived here in Oporto. We were told we were now the property of the duke. We were put to work once we were bathed and our sickness had passed. At first, we worked in the field behind the duke's palace. Then we worked in the laundry and kitchens. As we learned Portuguese and were able to carry on a simple conversation, we were questioned by the duke about our previous life in our town. He was most interested in our story of managing a dry-goods warehouse, and so he gave us a similar job. We worked in that capacity until we were replaced by other slaves. That was when he offered us to the Church."

Now, a month after Rodrigo received the sisters from the duke, he had made up his mind. Looking at the spherical astrolabe sitting on his desk, the priest thought back to when Vasco da Gama arrived back home to Portugal. Da Gama, extremely relieved that the voyage was accomplished safely, told Rodrigo that he was certain the credit belonged to the spherical astrolabe. "Father, I believe in Divine Providence, but I also believe Divine Providence brought you to me to guarantee the safety of my return home. Not only brought you to me, but brought this blessed instrument you gave me."

Father Rodrigo had not anticipated that da Gama would return the device to him. When he gave the device to him, he had hoped that the great admiral would continue to use it to ensure the safety of future voyages across the perilous oceans. But that was before Rodrigo learned that the Portuguese were now engaging in and promoting the slave trade in west Africa and were using slave labor in the colonies across the Great Ocean.

Fortunately, da Gama obtained several more spherical astrolabes in anticipation of his next voyages to Asia. No longer needing the device given to him by the priest, da Gama made a great occasion of handing back the spherical astrolabe.

Rodrigo had graciously accepted the device without any future plan for it. Now he had a plan. He told his housekeeper to ask the sisters to come to his study. When they arrived, they still wore their aprons and looked like they had been working in the kitchen. Khadijah spoke first, "Yes, Father. You wanted to speak with us?" She and her sisters remained standing.

"Yes, I would like to speak to you about something. But first, please sit and be comfortable." Father Rodrigo arose, walked to his bookcase and removed a large object. Turning around he carried the object carefully back to his desk and set it down. "I doubt you will know what this is, and certainly not what it has become."

Sofia leaned forward to get a better look. "It resembles a nautical device I caught a glimpse of in the duke's office. I don't know what it's called, though."

"It's a spherical astrolabe. The duke has several, and he tells me he used a different one on his last exploratory voyage to the Cabo Verde Islands. This one, however, belongs to me. As I said, it has become something different."

Maryam raised her eyebrows. "How so, Father?"

The priest turned to Khadijah and said, "Would you mind closing the door? What I'm going to tell you is for your ears only." He waited until

she had done so and returned to her seat. "You might have learned that before I returned home to Oporto, I was a parish priest for 40 years in Mogadishu, Somalia. Do you know where that is?"

Sofia and Maryam shook their heads but Khadijah nodded. "It's a city on the east coast of Africa. On the Indian Ocean, is what I've heard. But I know nothing about it. How did you travel such a long distance?"

"I was parish priest at Santo Condestável church in Mogadishu from 1460 to 1499. After that I was invited to serve as chaplain aboard Vasco da Gama's fleet, and did that from 1499 to 1500. This is how that happened. In January 1499, the fleet had anchored about a mile out from the Mogadishu harbor. It was on its way back to Portugal from a trading trip to India. While the fleet was anchored off shore, a local fishing captain transported myself and one of my parishioners to da Gama's ships. My parishioner presented this astrolabe to the Great Admiral as the fleet lay at anchor.

"A spherical astrolabe is a vast improvement on the traditional astrolabe used by mariners for hundreds of years. With this, da Gama understood he would be able to safely round the notorious Cape of Good Hope at the bottom of the African continent on his way home to Portugal from a successful trading trip to India. Sailing in that direction around the Cape was much more perilous than sailing from west to east, especially using a traditional astrolabe. In gratitude, da Gama granted my request to join the crew as ship's chaplain for the return voyage to Portugal. What da Gama did not know was that this particular astrolabe was different; it had been modified."

Sofia said, "You say this astrolabe is different, but it looks just like the one in Duke Àlvares's office."

Father Rodrigo lowered his voice and said, "What I'm about to tell you will surprise you. You will have trouble believing me. But be patient, because I have a plan for you three to gain your freedom; not only your freedom, but your return to your home in Mali."

The three ladies gasped and looked at one another. Khadijah said, "Father, I promise you we will be very attentive."

Rodrigo took a breath and launched into his story. "During my years as a priest in Mogadishu, I had become good friends with a man named Horacio Fuente, may he rest in peace. He told me remarkable stories of having arrived in Mogadishu from the distant future. Not only from the future but from a place I had never heard of—an island nation in the Pacific Ocean called `Hawaii.' Fuente showed me this spherical astrolabe here. According to Fuente, it had been converted into a time machine capable of transporting the user through time. Fuente said he ended up stranded in the past when a wire broke inside the astrolabe. He lived out the rest of his life in Mogadishu. He married and raised a daughter with his wife.

"In his old age, it was his dying wish that his daughter, Alessandra, present the astrolabe to the Great Admiral. Fuente's hope was that the device would eventually be used to change history."

The three sisters remained silent and looked at one another. Finally, Maryam spoke. "Father, I do not understand how one can travel through time except in the usual way, from birth to death. But you are saying that this machine can transport someone backwards through time. Is that right?"

"Yes, that is what I'm saying. I'm also saying that something inside this astrolabe, a wire inside this small golden globe here, broke."

Khadijah said, "And you propose somehow to repair the device? And what then?"

"Yes, repair it and then use it to send you ladies 54 years back in time to Niumi, the capital of the Mali Empire, to the year 1446. I have a plan. I've done a lot of research into that empire. And I think my plan will save west Africa from what has happened to the people there in the past 54 years.

"In 1446, the control of Mali was characterized by disputes among the regional rulers. The remaining center of power in Mali was the coastal city of Niumi, a city of 100,000 souls. But the city was frequently harassed after the eastern half of the country was conquered by Tuareg nomads from the north. Another threat to the Malians was the arrival of Portuguese slavers two years earlier in the year 1444. In response to those threats, a powerful family in Niumi installed Duke Gbèré Keita as the "Mansa." At first, Duke Keita was successful in driving off the Portuguese. But in the end, the Portuguese succeeded in subduing the coastal areas and obtaining countless numbers of slaves."

Khadijah said, "Yes, we know that history very well and the history of the beginnings of the slave trade with the Portuguese. We ourselves were taken into slavery in 1495 by the Portuguese."

"Yes, I am counting on your awareness of all those details."

Sofia said, "But assuming time travel is possible, how will our arrival back in time to 1446 change that?"

"My hope is that you will be able to block the advances of Portugal in Africa and ultimately to the Americas. Once you have arrived in Niumi, you must convince Duke Keita that his only hope of blocking the Portuguese scourge will be to destroy Portugal's power before they expand their slave trade off the coast of west Africa.

"This is my plan, which you should present to Keita: He must outfit a fleet of the local fishing boats, `pirogues', with sails and travel to the islands of Cabo Verde some 300 miles northwest of the mouth of the Gambia River. At that time those islands had not yet been discovered by Portuguese sailors. That discovery was in the year 1456 by a small fleet of three ships of a new design, `caravels,' commanded by Antonio de Noli, Alvise Cadamosto and Diogo Gomes.

"But upon your arrival in Mali 10 years before then, you must try to convince the Malians to travel to those islands in order to be ready for the arrival of the Portuguese. Duke Keita would have known about the islands from the legend of the sole surviving ship of a Malian fleet that had attempted to sail west across the Atlantic 100 years before. Keita will also have experienced the beginning of the Portuguese slave raids on the Malian coast in 1444."

Maryam frowned and said, "Pardon me, Father. Even if your machine sends us back to that time and place, how will Keita stop the Portuguese with a few fishing boats?"

"You will not make that voyage in a few fishing boats. If you are successful in convincing the Malians, you and they will travel to Cabo Verde in a fleet of dozens of the much larger sail-outfitted pirogues. You and the Malians will settle and fortify the islands. Then you will be ready for the arrival of the Portuguese.

"You will provide a proper welcome to the Portuguese. Historical accounts describe those three Portuguese caravels as armed with cannons, but having small crews—only a dozen men on each ship, mostly African slaves working as interpreters and sailors. After the crews come ashore to explore the islands, dozens of armed Malians will surround them and take them prisoner. Overpowering them should be easy, especially with the assistance of the enslaved Africans.

"For the next few months, with the assistance of the African crew members, you will learn to sail the caravels. Then it will be time to change history itself! Three full crews of Malians, including you sisters, will sail the Portuguese caravels north to Portugal and Spain to attack those Portuguese and Spanish ports before their ships can begin their predations of Africa."

Sofia asked, "And then what? Won't the Portuguese and Spanish simply build more ships?"

"It is my hope that the Malian attackers will be able to destroy the docks, the entire ship-building operations in Lagos, Portugal, and seize several more caravels. Then your expanded fleet will sail the short distance to Huelva, Spain, and destroy as much of that port as you can. Those two ports were where Cristoforo Colombo's fleet departed eight years ago and Pedro Cabral's fleet departed a little over a month ago. It is my hope that the destruction of those ports and seizure of the caravels will give the Malians enough time to fortify the Cabo Verde Islands and send a fleet of caravels across the Atlantic to the continents that otherwise would be claimed by Spain and Portugal."

Khadijah said, "I have heard of Colombo's voyage; his three ships landed at some islands on the other side of the Atlantic. Are you saying that Cabral's fleet also will land at those islands?"

"No, Cabral is sailing further south and will discover a vast continent there. That is the future that my friend Horacio described. In the history that Horacio knew, the Spanish and Portuguese discovered new continents across the Atlantic. They destroyed civilizations there, enslaved the native peoples, robbed them of everything of worth, and created colonies of Europeans. That disaster continued for centuries, according to my friend Horacio Fuente. I feel it is my duty to use every means I have to prevent that from happening. It is my hope that you three will enable the Malians to prevent the Spanish and Portuguese from embarking on their genocidal explorations. And that you will enable the Malians to fortify the indigenous peoples of the two continents on the west side of the Atlantic."

Sofia said, "But you said earlier that this device no longer functions. A wire is broken inside the little globe. How can it be repaired?"

Father Rodrigo said, "That is my worry—that perhaps this spherical astrolabe here, our time machine, cannot be repaired so easily, if at all. I hope to find someone in this city who might be able to make the repair."

Maryam said, "Father, you say the wire that passes through this little gold globe is broken. There is an elderly Frenchman who might be able to repair the device. He has a small jewelry shop in the middle of Oporto. His name is Gabriel Hugo, and he once lived in Paris." She turned to Khadijah and asked, "You met him once, didn't you?"

"Yes, I did. I delivered a gold necklace of Duke Àlvares's concubine for him to repair. He is quite elderly, as you say, but appears to be healthy."

Father Rodrigo asked, "Do you think he would consider coming to my office at the Church to examine the astrolabe?"

Khadijah said, "I can ask him, but you will have to request the duke's permission for me to leave the Church grounds. I imagine he would approve the request to repair your spherical astrolabe."

CHAPTER TWO

Gabriel Hugo closed his shop early, an hour after one of Duke Àlvares's slaves, a young woman he knew as Khadijah, had come to him with a request. She had asked if he would come to the Igreja de Santa Clara to meet with the pastor, Father Rodrigo. When she told him the nature of the visit—to repair a spherical astrolabe—Gabriel had a tingling feeling.

Gabriel told his housekeeper not to prepare dinner that night, as he would supp at the Church with the pastor. He walked slowly and painfully through the narrow cobblestone streets beside the city's Fernandine Walls, relying on his cane to avoid slipping in the dim light.

The mention of the spherical astrolabe brought him back to his days as a Parisian youth 82 years before. He had been a 10-year-old jeweler's apprentice in a section of Paris devoted to shops selling gems, gold, silver and other precious metals. His master, an eccentric genius named Nicolas Flamel, was known as a master in repairing nautical instruments such as astrolabes. He was less known as an alchemist.

For almost a month, Flamel had been working on a mysterious project that he allowed only Gabriel to assist him with. Gabriel had asked Flamel about the device, but all he said was that he hoped the device would be capable of "navigating the interstices of time itself!"

And finally, on the Spring Equinox, March 21, 1418, Flamel announced himself ready to set off on a voyage to the future. Gabriel was unsure what his master meant by that, but was eager to find out. "Master, what will be your destination?"

"Better to ask, 'when' will be my destination. I have prepared this machine"—pointing to the spherical astrolabe that sat on his work table—"to transport me to the past and to the future. I am most interested in learning what is in store for our wonderful, but ravaged, Earth. Perhaps I will learn a way to protect our beautiful Earth from a fate I have witnessed in my nightmares!"

What happened next Gabriel would never forget. He helped Flamel hoist a heavy, packed bag onto his shoulders. After Flamel adjusted the bag to sit comfortably on his shoulders, he turned to the table on which sat his modified astrolabe. He placed both hands on the ends of the arrow that passed through the astrolabe from bottom to top. And then—he and the spherical astrolabe simply disappeared!

Now, as Gabriel walked to the Church, the memory of that event stayed with him. Nicolas Flamel's words stayed with him for the rest of his life —"Perhaps I will learn a way to protect our beautiful Earth from a fate I have witnessed in my nightmares!"

Father Rodrigo greeted Gabriel at the rectory door and ushered him into the study. Inside, Gabriel saw the same young African woman who had come to his shop, as well as two other African women. As they stood up from the work table, the priest said, "Please, Master Hugo, allow me to introduce you to these young women—Khadijah, whom you have met already, and her younger sisters Sofia and Maryam. They work for the Church with Duke Àlvares's permission. Ladies, this is Master Gabriel Hugo. Khadijah tells me he owns a wonderful shop in town where he is renowned for his skill in repairing a variety of objects." Gabriel smiled and shook hands with the three women.

Gabriel noticed a spherical astrolabe sitting on the work table. "So, this must be the astrolabe. It doesn't look damaged, but Miss Khadijah says it is in need of repair."

"Yes, that's correct. But let us have our evening meal first. I can explain the situation as we eat." Everyone walked into the dining room, where a servant stood at the doorway to the kitchen. The dining table was set with a variety of dishes. The group sat down and Father Rodrigo said, "Please, let us not allow the food to get cold. We can talk as we eat."

At first the conversation was general. The women asked about Gabriel's shop and how long he had been in business. "I opened my shop a little over 40 years ago, after I had been living in Oporto about 10 years working for other craftsmen and jewelers."

Sofia asked, "And before coming to Oporto, where did you live? I detect a French accent."

"Yes, you are correct. I am French. I was born and raised in Paris. And you, young ladies, how do you find yourselves living in Oporto?"

Sofia glanced at Father Rodrigo, who gave a subtle nod for her to answer the question. "As Father Rodrigo said, we three are sisters. We were born and grew up in Mali, daughters of the chief of a village near the town of Jenne. Our village was raided by slave traders. We were kidnapped and taken to the slave auction at the mouth of the Gambia River. Our parents were killed, as were many others. The Church's benefactor here, Duke Àlvares, purchased us five years ago and of late has loaned us to Father Rodrigo to assist him at the Church." She sat silent for a moment waiting for Gabriel to register what she had said and to respond.

"Yes, I remember when Duke Àlvares returned from his exploratory journey along the coast of Africa. I am so sorry to hear about your tragedy. I have always condemned slavery as one of the worst of sins." Turning to Father Rodrigo he said, "What are your feelings about the subject? Or would this be a good time to discuss the matter of the astrolabe instead?"

The priest set down his wine and leaned forward. "Actually, the two matters are related." Dabbing his lips with his napkin, and then looking at each of the sisters, he turned back to Gabriel. "I don't know if you have ever heard of the idea of time travel, that is traveling through time at will instead of in the ordinary way, from birth to death. Well, my spherical astrolabe is what you might call at time machine."

Gabriel raised his eyebrows. After a long pause, "Indeed, I have heard of time travel. I once knew someone who claimed it was not only possible, but intended to venture through what he called the `interstices of time.'"

The priest took a deep breath and leaned back in his chair. The three sisters sat in stunned silence. Then the priest said, "Tell me more about this acquaintance of yours."

"Well, why don't I return tomorrow afternoon with the tools I shall use to repair your spherical astrolabe. While I work on the machine, I'll tell you something about my friend. Sometime after lunch?"

"That would be wonderful." After another few minutes of eating and chatting, Father Rodrigo saw Gabriel out and turned to the sisters. "Well, it looks like we can look forward to an interesting day tomorrow."

Gabriel had trouble sleeping that night. The sight of the spherical astrolabe excited him. It reminded him of the one Master Nicolas Flamel modified. Finally, Gabriel drifted off to sleep. But not deeply; he kept dreaming of that time in his youth when he apprenticed for Flamel. In his dream, he vividly relived the day the 78-year-old alchemist told 10-year-old Gabriel of his plan to fly through time to the far distant past and future.

But then Gabriel's dream shifted to an outdoor scene. He saw his master walking on a hot dusty road in Spain talking to a man who Gabriel's dream told him was a Jewish mystic named Abraham Zacuto, the royal astronomer for Portuguese King John II. As Flamel and Zacuto walked, Zacuto was describing his astrolabe made of copper. They also discussed the history of the world—the future history. Zacuto told Flamel about a talisman "that will free you from the astrolabe and give you long life" and described where to find one. Their conversation woke Gabriel up.

The next day, Gabriel had few customers so he decided to close up his shop early. He packed up several tools he thought he would need and left for the Church.

The priest's housekeeper answered Gabriel's knock at the rectory door and showed him into Father Rodrigo's study. The priest looked up from his desk. "Ahh, Master Hugo. I'm happy to see you in the afternoon instead of in the evening. Please, let us go to the work room; I'll have my housekeeper summon our three sisters."

Once everyone was seated around the work table, Father Rodrigo said, "Before I begin my story, why don't you examine the astrolabe?"

Gabriel picked up the device and turned it from side to side. "I hear a rattle inside the little globe. Is there something broken inside?"

"Yes, indeed. I'm hoping you will be able to repair it."

Gabriel said, "I'm sure I will." Then he focused on the end of the arrow that passed through the astrolabe from the bottom, through the gold globe in the center, and extended out the top. He gasped when he saw a small set of initials inscribed on the arrow.

The priest said, "What is it? What do you see?"

"I recognize this. It's a monogram of the two initials of my master's name, NF—Nicolas Flamel." He pointed to the bottom end of the arrow.

Father Rodrigo frowned. "Those are hardly visible at all. I had never noticed them. Nicolas Flamel—you mean the famous Catholic philanthropist from 80 years ago in Paris?"

"Yes. I was his apprentice when I was 10 years old."

The priest said, "I thought apprenticeships lasted seven years, ending at age 18. What happened? Did you misbehave?" Rodrigo chuckled.

"No, my master disappeared." This time it was his turn to chuckle.

"I remember reading about him. He didn't disappear. According to Catholic histories he died in 1418 or thereabouts."

Gabriel sighed, "No, he didn't die then. Although I'm aware of the official story. He disappeared. Right in front of my eyes."

Sofia looked over at her sisters. Khadijah said, "This sounds like magic. The legend of this man—if it's the same man—was known in my country, Mali. He was said to be a French alchemist who could create spells. Some said he was a magician. Are you saying he literally disappeared?"

"Yes. Right in front of my eyes."

The sisters looked at one another. Maryam said, "Please explain."

"Here's what happened. This machine here, this very spherical astrolabe, was modified by my master, Nicolas Flamel, the man who put his initials on the arrow. I helped him modify the machine. It took several weeks to obtain the necessary materials, and then another few days to complete the modifications. When he was satisfied the machine was ready, he shouldered a satchel, put one hand at each end of this arrow, and then it happened."

"What happened," the three sisters asked at the same time.

"Like I said, he disappeared. And the machine, too."

The three sisters sat silent. The priest frowned.

Gabriel said, "Okay. Now I'm going to tell you the rest of the story of my master's disappearance.

"Nobody knows what happened to Nicolas Flamel after he disappeared. One thing I knew, and his wife knew, was that he was not buried in Paris at the Eglise de Saint Jacques de la Boucherie, as his legend holds. He was married to Perenelle Flamel, a wealthy Parisian noblewoman. When my master disappeared, I immediately informed Madame Flamel what had happened. With the Church's permission, she arranged a private 'burial', with no witnesses, to avoid a scandal."

Father Rodrigo said, "But we do know what happened to this astrolabe, whoever modified it. According my time-traveling friend Horacio Fuente, it was found in the year 2018. It was inside a trunk in the attic of a mansion on an island called Hawaii in the Pacific Ocean. That island lies to the west of the great land mass called `America,' the continent discovered by Cristoforo Colombo eight years ago.

"I know this because the man who found this astrolabe was João da Gama, a colleague of Fuente's. They and other professors of history in Hawaii wanted to travel back in time to the year 1430, to Mogadishu, Somalia, a city on the coast of northeast Africa."

Khadijah interrupted. "But wait. Why northeast Africa, and why that year."

The priest said, "I can only tell you what my friend Horacio told me. I was the parish priest in that city. Horacio's group arrived from the future, each with a spherical astrolabe they had modified just like this one. According to Horacio, the group was interested in the history of east Africa and its relations with Asia. They explored the city for a few hours, but then became frightened by the presence of Chinese sailors from a nearby `Treasure Ship.' The professors knew from the history of those ships that the sailors were notorious for kidnapping various types of experts to assist as crew members. So, the professors fled from the sailors and returned to the future, 2018.

"All except for Horacio, who fell and broke something inside his astrolabe, this machine here. He couldn't find anyone in Mogadishu who knew how to repair the device. After that, he had no choice but to live out the rest of his life in Mogadishu. He married and became a member of my congregation."

Gabriel said, "So, you summoned me to repair this machine. But my question is why."

Father Rodrigo said, "It is my hope that this astrolabe will be able to transport these three sisters, stolen from Mali, west Africa, back to their home. But, God willing, they will arrive about 10 years before the Portuguese explorers will discover the Cabo Verde Islands off the Mali coast. Forty-four years ago, the first small Portuguese fleet discovered the islands in 1456. The fleet consisted of three caravels commanded by, respectively, Antonio de Noli, Alvise Cadamosto and Diogo Gomes. They were blown off course and inadvertently discovered the islands. Each caravel had a crew of no more than 10 men. They were full of supplies they intended to trade up the Gambia River." Turning to the sisters he said, "Why don't you explain the plan I presented to you last evening."

Sofia looked at Gabriel and said, "The Father's plan is that we three sisters will use this machine to travel back in time to 10 years before 1456 and prepare the Malians for the arrival of the Portuguese."

She paused and Maryam took up the narrative. "We'll have to convince the Mali rulers that there is a group of `undiscovered' islands 300 nautical miles west of Mali, islands that would soon be discovered by the Portuguese and named the Cabo Verde Islands. Our argument to the Malians would be that if they don't send a fleet of armed, sail-equipped, pirogues to those islands, and be ready to confront the Portuguese, the sad, tragic history of European enslavement of Africans will unfold and continue unabated. Even at that early date, the Malians were very troubled by the repeated slave raids on their coast. Those raids began in 1444, so our encouragement will focus on stopping those raids."

Gabriel said, "So, you hope to be ready to confront and defeat the Portuguese. How do you plan to do that?"

Khadijah said, "Dozens of armed Malians in pirogues will await them in a hidden inlet near the bay where the Portuguese ships will arrive. We will have constructed several simple huts on the shore where the ships will drop anchor. Inside each hut will be several armed Malian soldiers. My sisters and I will greet the Portuguese when they come ashore. Although the caravels will be armed with cannon, their crew members will be ashore.

"After the sailors have come ashore to greet us, the armed Malians will emerge from the huts to join our greeting party. The Malian soldiers will surround the Portuguese, disarm them, and prevent them from returning to their ships. Then the Malian pirogues will emerge from their hidden inlet and block their ships.

"Once the sailors are bound, we will take over their group of caravels. We anticipate that the African crew members will be slaves and will be willing to help us. We hope that a few weeks will be enough time for us to learn to sail the caravels with their assistance. During that time, more Malian colonists will arrive to fortify the islands.

"Once the islands are protected by our colonists, the three caravels, carrying dozens of Malians, including we three sisters, will travel to the ports of Lagos, Portugal, and Huelga, Spain. On that voyage, each caravel will transport three pirogues. The pirogues will be armed with lightweight swivel guns, a supply of lead ball shot and dozens of pots of flammable oil.

"The caravels will arrive at night, drop anchor some distance from the shore to avoid detection, and lower the pirogues to the water. Because the cannons aboard our caravels might not be within range of their ports and ship-building operations, it will be the task of the pirogues to move in closer and commence the attack on the ports. Malian rowers will row the armed pirogues closer to the ships and docks, and begin launching fire pots at the docks. Once the docks are burning, our caravels will move in within cannon range. We will fire our cannons at the docks and any defenders. We will attempt to capture as many caravels as we can and sail them back to Mali."

Gabriel raised his eyebrows. "Three questions come to my mind. First, how will you know where the Cabo Verde Islands are? How will you learn to sail a caravel? And how will you know how to find the ship-building ports?"

Father Rodrigo said, "I can answer that." He stood and walked to a book case, pulled two rolled-up maps off the shelf, and brought them back to the work table. Unrolling the first one, he pointed to a small group of half a dozen islands off the coast of Mali. "These are the Cabo Verde Islands, so named by the Portuguese. The Malians should be able to find them easily with this map. As for learning to sail a caravel, the new colonists will have plenty of time to do so."

Unrolling the second scroll he pointed to two ports off the coasts of Portugal and Spain. "The ship-building operations in Lagos, Portugal, and Huelga, Spain, are here. These two ports were where Colombo's fleet departed eight years ago, and the Portuguese Admiral Cabral's fleet departed a little over a month ago. You can see how poorly defended they are. They will not expect a fleet of armed caravels or a group of armed pirogues to attack them. It shouldn't be difficult to destroy the docks, the ships and the entire operation.

"After destroying the ports, the Malians will seize any undamaged caravels and sail them back to our Cabo Verde base. Using those caravels, Malian sailors will begin patrolling the African coast looking for Portuguese ships. The Malians will capture any they see, set the sailors adrift offshore on rafts, free the slaves and enlist the ships and slaves for the upcoming journey to Brazil. Even if the Spanish and Portuguese manage to rebuild, the Malians can pay them a return visit."

Khadijah said to Gabriel, "In the meantime, more Malian pirogues would have sailed to the Cabo Verde Islands to continue the fortifications and prepare to equip the captured caravels to sail to the vast continent off the southwest Atlantic."

CHAPTER THREE

Gabriel picked up his leather satchel from the floor and placed it on the table near the astrolabe. "Okay, it sounds like you have a plan. So, let's get started." He pulled out a half-meter long iron needle with a pointed tip at one end and a wooden handle at the other. He lit the priest's oil lantern and slid the astrolabe closer. Placing the needle's tip into the flame, he kept it there for several minutes until the tip was red hot. Then he inserted the needle between the bands on the perimeter of the astrolabe. He carefully slid the red-hot needle around the perimeter of the little globe inside until an opening became visible in the seam holding the top half to the bottom half. Then he slid the needle around the entry points on the top and bottom of the globe where the arrow passed through. "There, I have melted the seam and the arrow's entry points. The two halves of the globe may be separated."

Gabriel set down his needle on a plate and waited for his audience to respond. Father Rodrigo pulled the astrolabe and oil lamp closer to him so he could get a good look at what Gabriel had accomplished. "That seam was invisible before! Well, now it looks like it should be possible to open the globe enough to have access to the wire that passes through it."

Sofia said, "If you need someone with small hands to reach in and grasp the globe, I think I could manage it." At a nod from the priest, she gingerly inserted one hand inside the bands of the astrolabe, grasped the top half of the globe and gently separated it from the bottom half, exposing the broken wire inside. Then she slid the globe's top half further up the arrow, exposing the interior of the globe.

Father Rodrigo leaned forward and peered closely at the separated halves of the gold globe. "I see a bed of small, flat wires on the bottom of the globe. There looks to be some kind of gemstone sitting on top of the bed of wires, and a silver wire passing through the gemstone. I see the break in the wire after it passes through the gemstone. What kind of wires are those flat ones lying on the bottom of the globe? And what's the gemstone?"

Gabriel said, "The bed of wires are platinum wires. The stone is an emerald-green chrome tourmaline, extremely rare. When Flamel constructed this, he attached one end of the silver wire to the spot on the arrow where it entered the bottom of the globe. Then he pulled the silver wire through that side of the globe, threaded the wire through the gemstone, pulled the wire taut to lift the gemstone up off the bed of platinum wires, and attached that end of the silver wire to the silver arrow where it exits the top of the gold globe."

Leaning back, the priest turned to Gabriel and said, "I don't know why someone couldn't have opened this the way you just did, with a long needle and lamp."

Gabriel said, "My guess is that in Mogadishu in the early 1400's, there was no one who was familiar with how this type of astrolabe was constructed. Also, the seam separating the top and bottom halves of the gold globe was virtually invisible. In my case, of course, I was intimately familiar with astrolabes, especially this one right here."

For a few minutes the room was silent. Finally, Khadijah spoke. "Master Gabriel, how do you propose to reattach the two halves of the broken wire?"

Gabriel smiled, reached into his satchel again and removed a small cloth pouch. Opening it, he pulled out a coil of what looked like very fine wire and a pair of extremely thin leather gloves. "This is silver wire. I will cut a small section and hand it to Sofia. She will put on these gloves first. She will lift up one end of the broken wire that's inside the globe and hold one end of my silver wire against it. I will then touch the heated tip of my needle against that spot, which will melt my silver wire onto the wire inside the globe. Once my silver wire has cooled and hardened onto that end of the broken silver wire, she will lift up the other end of the broken wire, hold my silver wire against it, and I will do the same with my heated needle. You'll see that lifting up and reconnecting the ends of the broken wire will raise the gemstone off the bed of flat platinum wires lying on the bottom of the globe.

"At that point you will have a completed circuit inside the globe. After that, I can reseal the two halves of the globe with the needle, and the repair will be complete."

Gabriel cut a length of his wire and handed it to Sofia, who performed the operation exactly as Gabriel had described.

That done, Sofia withdrew her hands, Gabriel set his needle down on a plate, and everyone took a breath. Khadijah said, "It looks like it will hold." Turning to the priest she asked, "What now?"

Gabriel reheated his needle and resealed the globe. "The repair is done. Your little time machine is ready to fly."

Maryam looked skeptical. "Can you explain how the machine functions? What I mean is, why is it necessary that the stone here, the tourmaline, be raised above the bed of platinum wires?"

Gabriel said, "My master said that the tourmaline emits some sort of energy which, when sitting near, but not touching, the platinum wires, has an effect on time and space."

Maryam didn't look any less confused. Father Rodrigo said, "I'm sure the science behind this machine is beyond my comprehension as well.

"Well, before the machine is ready to fly, my three passengers must get ready to fly. Master Gabriel, I cannot thank you enough." Reaching into the drawer of the work table, he removed a small cloth pouch. He handed the pouch to Gabriel and said, "Here are 20 silver coins from the duke's own mint. I hope that will be sufficient."

Gabriel smiled, "It is more than enough. Thank you for your generosity." Turning to the sisters, he said, "And I wish you the best of luck on your journey."

Turning back to the priest, he said "I just remembered a very important piece of advice. Two pieces, actually. First, when the sisters are ready to embark on their journey, they will stand around the astrolabe and hold hands. One sister will place one hand on the tip of the arrow at the top of the astrolabe, while keeping her other hand in the middle sister's hand. At your signal, the third sister will grasp the bottom of the arrow with her free hand. That will complete the energy circuit between the top and bottom of the arrow, activate the astrolabe and send the sisters to their destination."

"And second, once you have arrived at your destination, you should immediately conceal the astrolabe inside a pouch so as not arouse suspicion, curiosity or greed. And you will need to dress in the type of attire common among the Muslim women of west Africa.

"Oh! First things first—destination! That is a very important thing that I almost forgot. You'll notice many geographic coordinates engraved on the outer, silver, band of the astrolabe. That band can be rotated so that a set of coordinates sits directly below the tip of the arrow. One set consists of the geographic coordinates for Mogadishu, Somalia, which I assume the Good Father's friend Horacio chose. You must rotate that outer band so that a different set of coordinates—presumably a location in Mali—will line up under the arrow's tip.

"Then, you'll notice the very narrow band that is directly below that outer band. That narrow band is made of platinum and was installed on this astrolabe by my master, Nicolas Flamel. You see the dates he etched on that band? You must rotate that band so that your desired date sits directly below your geographic destination, both of which will be below the arrow's tip."

Gabriel stood, stretched, and placed his tools back into his satchel. Turning to the three sisters he said, "I must leave you now; my housekeeper will be worried. I wish you luck!" Turning to the priest he said, "Father Rodrigo, this has been a most interesting assignment you have given me. Please do keep me informed as to the outcome."

The priest laughed and said, "Well, if this plan works, the world—especially Europe—will be a very different place that it is now!" Then he smiled, shook Gabriel's hand and said, "God willing, it will be a better world! Thank you and God bless you."

CHAPTER FOUR

After Gabriel left, Maryam turned to Father Rodrigo and said, "Father, something occurred to me just now when Master Hugo asked you to keep him informed after we embark on our journey to the past. If, as you have planned, we carry out our mission and change the course of history, what will happen to you? Or to Oporto? Or to the wealth of Spain and Portugal that has come from the new world? Colombo will never reach the new world, right? Nor will Admiral Cabral."

Father Rodrigo sat down at the work table and was silent. So were Khadijah and Sofia. "Those are very good questions." He arose again, rolled up the maps and returned them to the bookcase. Turning around, he said, "No need to try to answer those questions now. They will answer themselves. Tomorrow morning, we must get started."

As directed, Father Rodrigo's housekeeper woke him up just before dawn. The priest told him to waken the sisters and tell them to come to the work room as soon as they can be ready. He dressed quickly and went into the work room. The spherical astrolabe was sitting on the work table next to three shoulder bags.

The priest put the map of the Cabo Verde Islands and the maps of the Spanish and Portuguese ports into one of the shoulder bags. He retrieved three robes with hoods and laid them across the work table next to the other shoulder bags. Into one of those bags, he packed extra clothing. The empty shoulder bag lay next to the astrolabe.

The sisters arrived shortly after that. The priest said, "First, let's set your destination and year." He pulled the astrolabe closer and rotated the outer band to the geographic coordinates of Niumi, the capital of medieval Mali. Then he rotated the platinum band below that band so that the date of 1446 appeared directly below the geographic coordinates he had selected.

He turned to the three sisters and said, "Before you begin your journey, please put on the robes with the hoods covering your heads. Then put these bags on your backs. One bag contains the maps I showed Gabriel yesterday. One bag is for the astrolabe after you arrive at your destination. The third bag contains extra clothing."

Once the sisters were ready, the priest said, "Remember how Gabriel said to activate the spherical astrolabe. Khadijah, you will place one hand on the tip of the arrow that passes through the astrolabe. You will place your other hand in Sofia's hand. Sofia will place her other hand in one of Maryam's hands. Maryam, on my signal, you will place your free hand on the bottom of the arrow."

When the first two sisters had done that, Maryam held her free hand just below the bottom of the arrow and waited for the priest's signal. Three seconds later he gave the signal, and Maryam did as the priest instructed, touching her free hand to the bottom of the arrow.

Immediately the view of the golden sunrise out the rectory window turned two-dimensional and gray. The view undulated, and it seemed as if they were looking through wavy glass in an antique window. Then the view dissolved and reconstituted itself as a tunnel, and then as an alley, dark on one end and bright on the other.

The Year 1446

They were no longer standing in the Church rectory. They were standing in the alley they had seen with buildings on either side of them. The buildings appeared to be two stories high. At the back of the alley, they could see empty crates and carts. In front of them was a crowded street or walkway. They could hear a cacophony of sounds—shouting, laughing, music, braying of donkeys. They were halfway down the alley from the entrance.

Maryam said, "Sofia—put the astrolabe in this empty bag on my back. We should put our hoods over our heads and take a look at the street!"

Sofia did that and then said, "I hear different languages spoken—Fulani, Malinké, even Arabic! I think we're home!"

Khadijah took a step out of the alley and stood at the edge of the street. None of the people passing her even slowed down, let alone stopped. She looked to her left and gasped. "Look at the size of that mosque! Maybe we should enter and see if we can get some information from the imam."

Her two sisters walked up to the edge of the alley and looked out at the mosque. Maryam said, "What kind of information?"

Sofia said, "Let's just ask for directions to Duke Keita's offices."

Khadijah said, "Right." The sisters carefully walked out of the alley and toward the mosque.

The mosque was a massive, two-story group of at least five structures linked together in a large circle surrounding the main edifice, the sanctuary. It was quite beautiful and expertly constructed of brick. The sisters entered what looked like an office to the left of the sanctuary entrance. A heavy-set man was sitting at a large desk busily writing something. At the sisters' entrance he looked up. "Yes, how can I help you?"

Khadijah spoke. "Thank you sire. My sisters and I seek an audience with Duke Keita. We wish to discuss a very important matter with him."

The man at the desk raised his eyebrows, set down his pen and was silent for a moment before answering. "Now, this is very interesting. It seems the duke is expecting you. He is within his office in conference with someone. Please, follow me." He arose and walked into a hallway. At the end of the hall, he stopped at a large doorway, knocked and opened the door. He stepped halfway in and announced the sisters.

They heard a voice within the room. "Have them enter, Arash."

Arash opened the door wider and stepped aside. Khadijah entered first, followed by Sofia and Maryam. Two men sitting at a long table arose as the sisters entered. Khadijah gasped as she recognized one of them. Turning to Duke Keita she said, "We are very honored to be in your presence, Your Lordship. My name is Khadijah Soraya; these are my sisters Sofia Amina and Maryam Nazar."

"Welcome to Niumi." Pointing to the man sitting to his left he said, "This is my advisor, Master Flamel. He has told me a little about you. But very little. Only that you wish to discuss the security situation in Mali. Is that right? You have some plan in mind, is what he has told me."

The three sisters were stunned. Before they could reply, Flamel turned to Duke Keita and said, "Perhaps we should all sit before we discuss what these sisters have in mind." At Flamel's suggestion, Keita indicated three seats on the opposite side of the table. Everyone sat. Keita asked them to begin the discussion.

Khadijah introduced herself and her sisters, and then asked, "Master Flamel, how is it you have known of us and our mission? We only just arrived here and haven't met with anyone other than Master Arash. Although, even though I don't believe we have ever met, I think I somehow recognize you."

"Yes, you arrived today, and you are correct that you have seen me before, in Jenne, some years ago. I had been living there then." He turned to Keita and said, "My Lord, why don't we ask these sisters to enlighten us as to their proposal for ridding your glorious kingdom of the cursed Portuguese?"

Again, the sisters were speechless for a few moments. Khadijah then smiled, shook her head, and said, "First you say you have been expecting us. Now you seem to know our purpose in coming here to your kingdom."

Sofia said, "Your Lordship, Master Flamel is correct that we hope to convince you to mount a challenge to the Portuguese and rid our coasts of their presence. But our proposals are quite specific, and will involve many challenges and perhaps sacrifices."

"Challenges and sacrifices? But I'm informed that those are not insurmountable obstacles, and in the end will very likely restore peace to not only my kingdom but to all of West Africa as well. Is that correct?"

Maryam answered, "Yes, that is our hope. Let me just say by way of introduction that the incursions and raids of the Portuguese will not stop by themselves. They will only increase and become more brutal. But there is one way to stop them, and that will be to destroy their ship-building operation in Portugal itself. And that of the Spanish as well."

Now it was Keita's turn to remain silent momentarily. Then he turned to Flamel and said, "I have to say, Nicolas, when you first spoke of this, I was skeptical that three young women would come and make such a proposal." Turning back to the sisters, he asked, "Please continue. I look forward to learning how to protect Africa from the Portuguese."

Khadijah said, "Since Master Flamel seems to have such knowledge of the future, perhaps you will not be surprised to learn of the group of Atlantic islands two day's sail northwest of here."

"Yes, I have heard of them. Several generations ago, in the time of my predecessor Mansa Musa, Peace Be Upon Him, a large fleet attempted to cross the Great Ocean. But only one ship returned, and the captain spoke of this group of islands."

Khadijah continued, "Well, it might surprise you to learn that up to now, your people are the only people who know of them. But that will change. Ten years from now a Portuguese fleet consisting of three caravels commanded by, respectively, Antonio de Noli, Alvise Cadamosto and Diogo Gomes will be blown off course to the northwest of here. They will inadvertently come upon the islands and name them Cabo Verde."

Keita raised his eyebrows and asked, "So, exactly how do you know the plans of the Portuguese 10 years from now?"

Sofia answered, "I'm surprised your esteemed advisor, Nicolas Flamel, has not explained how our journey began and from whence we came."

Flamel smiled, turned to the king and said, "They have come from the future, My Lord. I gave them a gift, albeit not personally, and in a very round-about way. Do you wish a more detailed explanation?"

The king drummed his fingers on the table, arose, turned, and looked out the window. Then he returned to the table and said to Sofia, "You came from the future. But you are plainly Malian. You speak Fulani with a Jenne accent, as if it were your native tongue. You also speak Portuguese. I have many questions, but I will put them aside for the time being. Please continue."

After allowing Keita a few moments to digest what Khadijah had said, Sofia outlined the proposal created by Father Rodrigo.

When Sofia finished, Maryam said, "So, Lord Keita, I'm sure you will understand the strategy my sister has outlined. We have been informed by our former employer, Father Rodrigo, that your kingdom has sufficient resources to outfit such an expedition to those islands. And you will discover that the resources on those islands will richly reward your endeavor. During the 10 years before the Portuguese 'discover' the islands, you will have had ample time to begin establishing a Malian colony there, but a colony well hidden from the approach of ships."

"Please explain how a colony of hundreds of people, dozens of pirogues and dozens of buildings can be hidden from approaching ships." Lord Keita looked skeptical.

Maryam replied, "As Khadijah has said, in 10 years, three

Portuguese caravels will drop anchor at Santiago Island, the island nearest to the African coast. Quite by accident, as it happened. Historical accounts from that time say the ships were blown off course. The island is uninhabited, as are the other nine islands in the group. Fortunately, for our purposes, the Portuguese will drop anchor at the southern tip of a peninsula that blocks the view of a bay. The banks of the bay are heavily forested, as is most of the island. Our little colony of Malians will have confined their building efforts to the land on the far side of the bay behind the peninsula, well-hidden from view.

"Our benefactor, Father Rodrigo, created a masterful plan. Three huts will be constructed on the peninsula where the Portuguese ships will anchor to investigate the island and replenish their supplies of food and water. As the crew rows ashore in their dinghies, they will see an acre of beans beside the huts. They will see half a dozen women in that field picking beans and putting them into baskets. Once all the crew members are ashore, the women will walk toward them as if to greet them. Instead, they will take knives out of their baskets and warn them to stop. Half a dozen armed Malian soldiers will emerge from each of the huts and take the sailors prisoner. Then, two heavily armed pirogues will emerge from the bay and block the sailors from returning to their caravels."

Keita's look of skepticism remained unchanged. "I see. And after taking the sailors prisoner, we will take possession of three armed caravels with which to challenge the hegemony of the European powers. I eagerly await your explanation of how we will learn to sail caravels, let alone enlisting the crew to teach us."

Khadijah smiled and said, "Well, don't forget, we will have 10 years to prepare our European surprise!" She turned to Maryam and said, "My sister, why don't you remove the maps from your pack."

Maryam took her pack off, removed the maps, unrolled the map of the Cabo Verde Islands and spread it out on the table. Flamel, Keita and Maryam's sister approached the table. Maryam asked the duke and Flamel to hold down the ends of the map. "The map shows the group of islands to the west of the African continent." Pointing to one of the islands she said, "This island here is closest to the African coast where the Gambia River flows out into the sea. In the future whence we came, the Portuguese, when they discovered the islands, named the islands Cabo Verde. They named this island here Santiago. That is where we should establish our greeting party for the Portuguese crews. Once we have taken them into custody, perhaps we shall put them to work clearing more land.

"We know from our study of history that the crews on those ships were Africans, taken as slaves from a previous raid on the coast. Those crews will assist us in learning to sail the caravels. Then we shall put the second part of our plan into play—sailing north to destroy the Portuguese and Spanish ship-building operations."

The meeting came to an end, and Keita escorted the sisters and Flamel into a small, intimate dining room where they had a leisurely lunch. Keita said to one of the staff, "Please inform Arash to arrange for the sisters to lodge here in one of the mosque auxiliary buildings." Turning back to Khadijah, he said, "Tomorrow, we shall meet here again and go over the details of this grand plan you have presented."

In the morning, before the sisters were called in for the meeting with Keita, they walked out into the courtyard to admire the garden. They were surprised to see Flamel bending over to examine one of the rose bushes. When he heard their approach, he stood and turned to face them. The sisters greeted him and he returned the greeting. Maryam noticed an amulet hanging on his chest and asked, "Master Flamel, that is a beautiful jewel. What is it?"

Flamel smiled and held the amulet in his hand.

"I've never seen anything like that!" Khadijah said.

"I acquired this from the treasury of Emperor Charlemagne 400 years ago. It originally belonged to the 9th century Caliph Harun al-Rashid of Palestine."

Sofia asked, "Did you use a spherical astrolabe to travel to that time?"

Flamel smiled and said, "Oh, indeed I did. It was my first trip to the past. Before I deposited my astrolabe in Hawaii six centuries from now—the very same astrolabe you three used in coming here."

The sisters stared at Flamel. Khadijah said, "Then the story we heard from Master Gabriel is true."

"Master Gabriel? What did the young master tell you?"

"He was not so young when we met him. He said that some 80 years earlier he had been your apprentice, and witnessed your invention of a time machine."

"Ah, yes, there is quite a story there, I must say."

Khadijah said, "But, Master Flamel, how is that you are now able to travel through time without the astrolabe you modified?"

"Well, it was always my hope to be able to continue my travels without having to rely on that bulky machine. In my historical research into the science of alchemy, I learned of a very potent talisman that contained a strand of hair from the Virgin Mary. It had been in the possession of the Caliph I mentioned just now, who presented it to Emperor Charlemagne. So, I paid a visit to the emperor's treasury and was able to acquire the gem. I won't bore you with the details of how I acquired it, or how it became a time machine."

Maryam said, "And I'm sure we wouldn't want to bore you by relating Father Rodrigo's experience to you. Later perhaps we will, but for now, time is short."

Khadijah said, "On that note, let us go inside and discuss our plans with Duke Keita."

The group spent most of their time at breakfast listening to Keita as he discussed the size of his fleet of pirogues, and to a lesser extent the route they would take to the coast. "It is not far to the coast by boat on the Gambia River, but first we must go on horseback to the river itself. There, we will board sail-equipped pirogues. By nightfall we should arrive at our capital city of Niumi at the mouth of the river."

When they had finished eating, they made their way to the stables and contemplated their choice of horses. Keita's groom suggested smaller horses for the sisters, but they protested. "You needn't worry about us. We grew up riding horses, and we are not afraid to ride at speed." Keita, Flamel and the sisters each chose a mount, and the duke's two bodyguards chose their mounts.

With Keita leading the way, the group began the two-hour ride to the river. It was slow-going at first because they had to ride through the western end of a rain forest. But when they finally emerged onto the plain, they were able to ride more quickly to the Gambia River.

Once there, the duke arranged stabling for the horses. Then he chose a large, sail-equipped, pirogue for the sisters, Flamel and himself, and their fast trip downriver began. The stable master had supplied them with simple food for the trip. As the wind and current propelled them downstream, there was no need to employ the oars. Keita said, "Be careful not to put your hands in the water. This river, which looks so beautiful, is full of animals of various sorts. Some of them, like crocodiles, snakes and hippos, are very dangerous. Once we arrive in a few hours, I will show you my docks and shipping operation. Niumi is one of the few places in my dukedom that is not under any threat by neighboring enemies."

CHAPTER FIVE

It was dusk when they arrived. The main channel of the river had not petered out at the coast but had forced its way out into the Atlantic Ocean. Along the south bank of the river, half a mile east of the mouth, lay numerous warehouses, workshops and wood-milling operations. They climbed out of the pirogue and Keita led them to the edge of a vast grassy area facing the river to the north. "This is where we make our pirogues of various sizes and uses. Fish are plentiful off shore, and pirogues are the best boats for fishing. The one we rode in today is one of medium size. We have made some twice its size."

Khadijah asked, "Your Lordship, do your workshops manufacture weapons as well?"

"Certainly. Cannons, rifles, firepots, and swivel guns, and a variety of lead shot and balls. We have large deposits of iron and lead half a day's journey inland."

Maryam asked, "Where are your sails made? Do you make them here? I see several smaller pirogues outfitted with them."

"Indeed, we do. There are fields to the south where we grow cotton for the sails. So far, we have not ventured far out into the ocean. I believe that to make the expedition you have described we would need to make much larger sails to outfit the largest pirogues." Turning to Flamel he asked, "What would an expedition to those islands be like? How long? What are the currents and winds like once the expedition is far enough away from the river current flowing into the sea?"

Flamel chuckled. "Well, My Lord. I may be wise but I am not possessed of infinite knowledge."

Khadijah interrupted. "Pardon, Master Flamel, but Father Rodrigo provided us with answers to those questions. The maps he provided us show the currents near the islands in some detail. They also provide estimates of wind direction and velocity at different times of the year. It was a school of Portuguese map makers who prepared these beautiful maps. So, I suppose we should thank them once we take their compatriots into custody!"

The Year 1448

"My Lord, the boats and crews are ready."

"But are the cannon and swivel guns correctly installed on the boats? Have they been tested sufficiently? Have extra boats' sails been stowed aboard. Does each captain have a copy of the maps?"

"Yes, sire. Everything is ready. Shall I give the order that we set out at first light?"

"I assume the crews have taken the boats out to test them?"

"Yes, My Lord. Each of the three boats is seaworthy. Shall I give the order?"

"And tell me again how many soldiers can be transported."

"My Lord, these pirogues are the largest we have ever constructed, and each can transport a dozen soldiers or workers, plus three sailors. These three boats, however, will only transport workers and materials to begin constructing docks, housing and other buildings. Our second fleet of three boats will set out a few days after the first. Shall I give the order?"

The duke sighed, smiled at Flamel and the three sisters, and said, "Yes you may. Wake us an hour before."

The fleet commander saluted and walked back outside. Flamel closed the door and asked, "Sofia, Maryam and Khadijah, I hope you are ready for this voyage. I know you have gone out in smaller pirogues several times, but not as far as the Cabo Verde Islands! The ocean can be very rough at times, although we are not expecting bad weather for at least the next week or so."

Khadijah answered, "Yes, Master Flamel, we are quite ready. Frankly, we are tired of waiting to begin this voyage. Anticipation is making us more nervous than the thought of making the trip."

Keita said, "I know we've gone over this before, but assuming good weather and favorable winds and currents, how many days will we be subjected to living aboard those pirogues?"

Flamel smiled, "If we set out at first light, we should reach the closest island, Santiago, in two days. Our pirogues are outriggers with enormous sails, as you have seen, and when full of wind those sales are capable of propelling the boats more quickly than smaller pirogues. I believe the larger size is an advantage, as it renders the boats more stable."

Maryam looked thoughtfully at the duke for a moment before asking, "My Lord, I know you've thought of this question, but please, I hope that you'll not be leaving your domain in a weak position from a defensive point of view."

Keita smiled, "I have every confidence in my army. They are loyal and battle tested. And they absolutely detest those malcontents on the northern borders of my land. You needn't worry. Anyway, I shall be returning to the mainland a month or so after the second fleet arrives. I am eager to set the first stage of the colonization plan in motion. But once it is underway, I must see to the outfitting of a third fleet. I may or may not accompany that fleet back here; it depends on the security situation at home."

Flamel's estimate was correct—the three pirogues dropped anchor at Santiago Island in the late afternoon of the second day. They had not encountered rough seas, and the winds favored them. The duke, Flamel and the three sisters rode in the lead pirogue. They were astounded at how fast the ships ran before the wind.

They approached a small sandy beach at the southern tip of a short peninsula and rowed the pirogues up onto the sand to inspect them for damage. To the south of the tip, they thought they could see what looked like the opening of a large bay.

After everyone had finished inspecting the pirogues for damage, the captain of the lead pirogue said, "Lord Keita, I recommend that I and my crew take this pirogue into the bay and do a little exploring. We won't be long." The duke nodded.

The crew pushed off and rowed until the wind filled the sail and pushed the pirogue toward the tip of the peninsula. After two hours, the pirogue returned and its crew rowed it up onto the sandy beach. The captain reported to the duke that the bay was quite large. "A river of good width flows into it. The bay is extremely well hidden from view. I believe it is quite possible to shelter a fleet of six ships in the bay. Many buildings could be constructed there."

On the duke's order, the three pirogues pushed off and proceeded around the tip of the peninsula and into the bay. What they saw astounded them. "Magnificent," Khadijah said. "The bay is almost completely circular!" Thick forest covered the land as far as the eye could see, with the trees marching down to within 50 yards of the water's edge.

The duke ordered the captain of the lead boat to take soundings in the bay to determine whether caravels could safely enter the bay. Once that was done, the captain reported, "This bay appears to be more than three Arabic fathoms deep at the shoreline and even deeper in the middle of the bay. Caravels should be able to drop anchor at the shore itself and offload supplies and equipment over a gangplank."

The duke gave the order for the sailors to row the pirogues up onto a broad beach. Khadijah said, "Lord Keita, I suggest that while most of us are unloading the boats, several of the more able-bodied men should begin cutting trees for shelter, piers and the like. Others perhaps could begin fishing from dinghies."

The Year 1452

When the fourth fleet of the massive pirogues arrived, they transported mostly men skilled in lumber work, women skilled in extending trails deep into the forest surrounding the bay, and men and women skilled in carpentry and iron work. Duke Keita, who had returned to the mainland the year before to make sure all was secure, was aboard this fleet and was eager to see what progress had been made on the "village" the Malians had made. It was his first trip back since the colony began taking shape.

When he came upon Maryam sitting atop the roof of one of the new buildings, he said, "I must say these buildings look quite a bit more substantial than the shacks you're planning to construct on the beach on the peninsula!"

"Of course. This will eventually be a village of substantial size, stretching well back into the forest. Those 'shacks' as you call them must be built to look like primitive dwellings to the Portuguese sailors when they arrive."

Keita smiled. "Only four more years! I'll wager everyone in this colony is looking forward to that!"

"Well, yes and no. Certainly it will be exciting, but also dangerous. We really don't know with any certainty how many crewmen will be aboard those three caravels. Father Rodrigo read varying accounts of the Portuguese landing. The more reliable accounts, however, said the crews consisted of a captain and 10 to 12 sailors on each ship. We do know who the three captains will be—Antonio de Noli, Alvise Cadamosto and Diogo Gomes. Some of the crewmembers will be Africans taken as slaves earlier when the ships went up the Gambia

River, others might be indentured Portuguese working off their debts. Most of the holds will be filled with goods to be traded upriver."

Keita said, "Well, with this latest shipment of goods we've brought quite a supply of weapons. The final group of pirogues will be sent here in three years, and it will be transporting several dozen soldiers. We'll be expecting the Portuguese to arrive less than two months later."

CHAPTER SIX

The Year 1456
August

"Commander Cadamosto, look where this storm has brought us! A heavily forested island!" As the clouds cleared, they could make out an island about a mile away. Cadamosto could see a peninsula extending south from main part of the island. He gave the order to make for the tip of the peninsula, and signaled to the other two caravels to follow.

When the three ships were safely anchored in a small harbor on the peninsula, Cadamosto said, "We'll make for that broad beach and explore the island. Perhaps, God willing, we shall find fresh water and wild game for meat." Four dinghies from each ship were lowered and the captains and crew members boarded them.

As the dinghies approached the beach, the sailors could see three shacks set well back from the beach. There was a small cultivated field to the right of the shacks. One of the sailors said, "I see a dozen women in that field holding baskets. They appear to be picking vegetables."

Captain Gomes chuckled and said, "Well, well, it looks like in addition to water and wild game, we'll have a different type of 'game' to enjoy!"

Once the captains and crew had disembarked from their dinghies, they walked ashore with the captains leading. The women walked toward them, smiling as if they were about to greet them. Instead, when just a few feet away from the captains, the women took long knives out of their baskets and pointed them at the men. One of the women was Khadijah, who spoke in clear Portuguese, "In the name of His Lordship Keita of Mali, I order you to stop and raise your hands. You are under arrest for violating his sovereign territory. Your ships and their contents are forfeit." The captains and sailors complied. A moment later, half a dozen armed Malian soldiers emerged from each of the three huts and approached. Khadijah continued, "You will be taken prisoner. You will not be harmed unless you resist. I warn you, do not resist or it will be the last thing you do!"

As she spoke, two heavily armed pirogues emerged from the bay. As soon as Captain Cadamosto saw them, he lunged at Khadijah, spun her around and pulled her knife out of her hand. He wrapped one arm around her, pinning her arms against her torso, held the knife up in the air, and said to her, "Order everyone to drop their weapons or I'll kill you!" Khadijah said nothing. At that moment, one of the African crew members lunged at Cadamosto from behind, wrested away the knife, and plunged it deep into his back, killing him instantly. The African threw the knife to one of the other Africans, who used it to stab Antonio de Noli. Diogo Gomes pulled out his knife and ran toward Khadijah. Maryam intercepted him and plunged her own knife deep into his chest, killing him. The African who had killed Cadamosto threw the knife to the ground and raised his hands in the air. Khadijah picked up his knife. She turned to the crew and shouted. "Surrender or you will soon be as dead as your captains! On the ground! Face down! Arms out! Now!"

That was enough for the crew. Each one of them, six Portuguese and nine Africans, complied with her order. Then the armed Malians went from man to man and bound their hands. Khadijah approached the African sailors who had killed Cadamosto and de Noli, she said,

"Turn over. That was very brave of you two. Are you crew or slaves?"

The first man said, "Both, my lady. All of us Africans are from villages up the Gambia River." The man who had killed de Noli said, "We were taken last year and have been working on these caravels as crew under Commander Cadamosto and others. These Portuguese crewmen are former inmates of debtor's prison in Oporto. They were chosen as crewmen to work off their debts. They will not mourn the deaths of the captains. They detested them and all the other nobles in Portugal."

"Tell me your names, the names of the other Africans, and the villages you came from."

"My lady, we are all nine from villages near the town of Jenne. My name is Hassan." Pointing to de Noli's killer, he said, "This is Kareem. The others are Salman, Adil, Yousef, Moussa, Ibrahim, Issa and Khalil."

By that time, Maryam and Sofia had come up to assist Khadijah and had overheard the conversation. Khadijah exclaimed, "We three are sisters who grew up near that town! Answer me truthfully—do you swear to assist us here on this island and never work for the Portuguese again?"

Hassan and Kareem nodded and swore. Khadijah asked the same question of the other Africans, and each of them swore an oath.

Then Sofia asked, "One more question—what were your jobs on board, and do you know how to sail a caravel?"

Maryam laughed and said, "That's two questions, Sofia." Turning to Yousef and the other Africans, she said, "So, what skills do you have?"

Yousef said, "We all know how to do everything on board these caravels. We have become skilled sailors."

Khadijah ordered six of her Malian soldiers to join her and her sisters and said to the African sailors, "Stand and walk in front of us to that shack on the left. You can sit in front of it." She said to another six of the armed Malian soldiers, "Guard these Portuguese crewmen." The nine African sailors walked to the shack and waited for her to speak.

Khadijah told Hassan to describe the tasks he performed on board the caravels. Hassan said, "We all learned most of the tasks on board—carpenter, boatswain, cook, gunner, cleaning the decks."

She asked, "But do you actually know how to sail one of those vessels?"

"Indeed, we do, my lady. Each of us learned to work in tandem with the Portuguese. What did you have in mind?"

"We are planning on a voyage to Portugal and Spain, a surprise visit you might say, to put an end to Europe's predatory practices in Africa. We plan to destroy their shipping industry.

"But come, let us go aboard one of your caravels now and you can show us what you know." Khadijah said to the six Malian soldiers who were guarding the Portuguese sailors, "Bind these men separately and strip them of all outer clothing. Stand guard over them." Turning to the six Malian soldiers standing with her, her sisters and the Africans, she said, "Follow us on board that caravel there. These men say they are our loyal compatriots and I'm inclined to believe them." She turned to the three dead Portuguese officers and said to the rest of her Malian soldiers, "See if you can find a suitable place to bury these men.

"So, I thought you would have furled the sails," Maryam said to Yousef as the group were about to explore the caravel before raising anchor.

"No need to, my lady," Yousef said. "The winds are not strong here in this sheltered cove where we had dropped anchor." Yousef and Hassan began leading the tour as the other sailors prepared to get underway. The tour began at the quarterdeck—a raised, open deck at the stern. Yousef pointed out the ship's wheel, along with a davit for the ship's boats.

Next the group went to the forecastle deck—a raised, open deck atop the forecastle. Hassan pointed out the cannon. After that, the group walked to the starboard side where the hawsepipe was and where the tackle for the ship's anchor was stored.

Then the group descended to the main deck, an open deck featuring a catapult and two companionways that descended to the lower deck. Yousef explained that the catapult could only be fired to the broadside. "It can't be aimed forward or back." He pointed out chicken coops and pens where goats, lambs and other small livestock were kept. Below the main deck was the forecastle. "Most of the ship's crew sleeps here in bad weather, although in good weather the men prefer to sleep on the open decks. The forecastle holds a dozen cramped bunks."

The group descended one level, and various crewmen pointed out the officers' cabins, the ship's office and a storage area for cargo. The next level down was the sail locker, "where spare sails, canvas, and sewing gear are stored, as well as plenty of lines, hawsers, firewood, and heavy tools." Finally, they descended to the lower hold. "Most of the ship's cargo is stowed here, as well as provisions and as many casks of fresh water as will fit. Beneath this lower hold, there is a small crawlspace where we keep heavy ballast stones help to stabilize the ship."

Yousef and Maryam stayed in the lower hold with a soldier to examine the goods stored there. The rest of the group went back to the main deck, and Hassan raised the anchor. Then he, Kareem and Salman took charge at the helm and showed Khadijah and one of the soldiers how to begin steering the ship around the tip of the peninsula. Khadijah took a turn at the wheel as she described the bay they would see and the progress of the Malian settlement there.

When Yousef, Maryam and the soldier were finished in the lower hold, they rejoined Khadijah, Kareem, Salman and the other Malian soldiers at the helm. Maryam reported, "The holds are packed with goods that the Portuguese had intended to sell or trade for other slaves up the Gambia River!"

Yousef said, "Many of the goods and items of clothing are of Portuguese manufacture, some are foodstuffs like grain, and others are farming implements of iron. I'm sure your colony here will find it all quite useful."

Maryam said, "Indeed we shall. The livestock on board will also be very welcome as breeding stock and meat."

Half an hour later, when the caravel had rounded the peninsula and entered the bay, all the sailors were on the deck with the sisters and the soldiers. The sailors were astounded at the number, size and variety of the structures that the Malians had built around the bay. A communal farm of more than 80 acres stretched far back from the shore. A dozen communal homes were spaced around the bay. A large factory was on one side of the bay and a lumber mill on the other. A fenced pasture full of sheep and goats was adjacent to the farm. And at the very end of the bay was a stockade. Adil and Khalil asked at the same time, "What are your plans for the prisoners?"

Khadijah turned and said with a frown on her face, "We have to decide. They may be too dangerous to set free to work for us. But you say they're former inmates of the Oporto debtors' prison who were released to work on the ships. What do you think? Would they be trustworthy workers here, say on the farm or in a factory?"

Khalil said, "I think you could allow them, separately, to work under supervision in the fenced pasture and barns with the animals. Not in the open field, certainly, nor in a factory. We worked with all the crew, obviously, and we got a pretty good idea of their character. We can help you decide on what to do with them. Some of them might be assigned to work cleaning out stalls and such, under supervision of course."

Sofia said to Khadijah, "We need to go back and retrieve the other caravels." Then she turned to Khalil and asked, "Do the caravels already have names?"

"Yes, but Catholic saints' names, of course. Santa Clara, Santa Beatriz and Santa Antonina."

"Well, that won't do! We need to rename them—give them Malian names!" She smiled and said, "I have some better ideas for naming the ships; women's names, of course. Here are a few I've thought of: Maimuna, Aminata, Halima and Adama."

Maryam said, "I love that idea! Let's put our heads together and rename the ships."

CHAPTER SEVEN

The Year 1459
November

During the past three years, the sisters had been busy learning to sail the caravels and planning their assault on the ship-building operations in Portugal and Spain. An assault on the Huelga, Spain, shipbuilding operation would proceed only after the assault on the port in Lagos, Portugal was successfully concluded. The final plan was that the three caravels would set out for Portugal at dawn on the 21st of that month. The sisters had decided that each of them would sail on a separate ship as Chief Mate under an experienced Gambian as Captain. Hassan would captain the "Fatouma" with Khadija as Chief Mate, Kareem would captain the "Oumou" with Sofia as Chief Mate, and Yousef would captain the "Aissata" with Maryam as Chief Mate. Khalil, Adil and Salman would each be Second Mate on the ships, and the three other Africans would be Mates. Each caravel would have 24 additional crew chosen from the Malian soldiers.

The week before their departure had been devoted to thoroughly inspecting the ships for seaworthiness, loading the ships with cannon balls and supplies, and installing on each ship two pirogues fitted with oars for eight men. Two lightweight swivel guns had been installed on each pirogue, along with a supply of lead ball shot, a catapult and dozens of pots of flammable oil.

Khadijah, Maryam and Sofia had already discussed and modified the attack plan several times with the crews. Now it was time to go over the final plan.

"The voyage will likely take a month or longer, depending on the winds and weather. Our three caravels will arrive at Lagos Harbor at night and drop anchor some distance from the harbor to avoid detection. From that distance the cannons aboard our caravels will probably not be within range of their port buildings and ship-building operations. That's where the six, armed pirogues come into the plan. They will be lowered into the water and rowed into the harbor.

"Hassan and the others tell us there will be numerous caravels tied up at the docks. The crews will most likely be ashore celebrating Christmas in bars, dance halls, or their homes. As each eight-man pirogue approaches a docked caravel, six of the men on each pirogue will slip into the water, leaving two on board for the moment. The six men in the water will climb onto a caravel and overpower any sailors present. Six men will be sufficient to sail the caravel out of the harbor to our fleet.

"At that point, the remaining two men in each of the six pirogues in the bay will begin launching fire pots at the docks. Once the pirogues have sufficiently damaged the docks, they will return to our caravels. Sailors on the caravels will then raise anchor and sail into the bay within cannon range. We will fire our cannons at the shipbuilding operation and other buildings on shore."

The assembled crew members digested the information. Nicolas Flamel said to the group, "I will not be joining you, as there is much work to be done here on this island before we begin work on the other islands." Turning to Salman, he asked, "You nine have made this voyage to Portugal once before, is that correct?"

"Yes. After we were taken as slaves and worked as crew on these three caravels, we sailed to Portugal. We were returning to Gambia when the weather blew our fleet off course to these islands."

"So, you know that you'll be traveling that distance again." Flamel turned to the rest of the Malian crew and said, "Be prepared to live aboard the vessels for almost a month, maybe longer if the weather is bad. Remember to avoid the Canary Islands; the Spanish have been colonizing them. You will deal with them on your way back home.

"When you approach Portugal, remember that you should plan on arriving at night to avoid being seen. I must warn you to avoid being seen by any ships as you approach Portugal. If you encounter another ship, you might have to attack it unless it is sailing away from Portugal. But even if it is sailing away from you, you must be wary and keep an eye out for it. Obviously, you must attack it if it pursues you."

Khadijah added, "I would add that even if our fleet is spotted as it approaches Portugal, our flags will be those of Portugal. It is unlikely we will be pursued; any observers would assume we are returning from a successful trade expedition to Africa. Nevertheless, we are prepared to fight if necessary. Once we are near our destination in Portugal, we will change our sails to those with Spanish markings as we prepare for our `Spanish attack' on the Portuguese port."

Maryam asked, "Master Flamel, what is the status of your plan to develop the remaining Cabo Verde Islands and secure them as a further bulwark against colonization?"

"We are making good progress. We anticipate another fleet of three large sail-equipped Malian pirogues to arrive in three weeks. Two of them will then sail to the nearest island, to the northeast of this one, with sufficient men and supplies to start developing it as a base. We also hope of course to obtain a few more caravels after the attacks on the Portuguese and Spanish harbors. The remaining workers, including the Portuguese prisoners, will have much to do on this island."

The ships did not encounter any bad weather or other ships as they sailed to Portugal. They stayed together and kept well away from the Canary Islands, which they planned on attacking on their way back "home" to Cabo Verde.

By nightfall on Christmas eve, they dropped anchor outside the Port of Lagos and waited for the deepest part of the night. It was heavily overcast and moonless. "How long do you think it will take our pirogues to row to within sight of the piers and docks?" The captain of one of the pirogues on the Fatouma was overseeing its lowering to the water.

Hassan said, "Depending on how fast you row and how strong the current is, it shouldn't take you more than an hour. Remember, the first objective is that six of the men on each pirogue will board and capture a caravel. In my experience, when my ship docked here on Christmas of last year, at least a dozen caravels were at anchor in the harbor. And there was no crew on any of them; everyone was ashore celebrating Christmas and a successful voyage to Africa. You shouldn't have any trouble boarding them in silence and overpowering any sailors on board. In all likelihood, there will be no one on board, and even if there is, he will most likely be passed out drunk or asleep."

"And if he's awake? What then? Do we kill him?"

"I doubt that will be necessary. Remember, any sailor ordered to stay aboard the ship while the others are ashore will most likely be an African slave. I'm sure you will be able to convince the man to join you!"

Once the two pirogues from each ship were launched, there was little for the caravel crews to do but wait and peer into the darkness. But the crews on the six pirogues were very tense as they rowed into the bay. After they had entered the bay, they fanned out. The crew of each pirogue headed for a specific dock where they could see a caravel tied up. Then, as each pirogue came closer to its target, the rowers stopped rowing. Six of the crew on each pirogue slipped into the water and swam the short distance to the caravel. The other two members of each pirogue waited to begin their role in the operation.

One by one, the swimmers climbed up the rope ladders of the ships and onto their decks. They were relieved to find that Hassan's prediction was mostly accurate—no sailors were aboard four of the six docked caravels, and on each of the other two there was only one sailor on the ship, who was lying on the deck passed out asleep or drunk. Siaka, one of the Malian sailors who boarded one of those ships, could see that the guard on that ship was an African. He shook him awake but immediately said, "Quiet! We are come to rescue you." Siaka held the man down and warned him not to struggle. "We intend to take this ship. There are six of us on board. Do you wish to join us, or shall I throw you overboard?"

The man relaxed and said, "I'll join you, but where are you going, and why are you here?"

"First, we shall destroy the docks and as many buildings as we can. Then we shall take this caravel and the five others in this harbor and rejoin our fleet offshore. After a few more operations like this, we intend to return to our home in Mali."

"Mali! That is my home as well. My name is Awolu. I and a dozen others were taken and forced to work on a sugar cane plantation on an island several days south of here. Half of them remained there while the Portuguese chose several of us to assist in their trip here. Certainly, I would rather join you!"

"Well, Awolu, to be certain of your new loyalty to us, I will have to keep you confined until we rejoin our fleet. Then you'll be questioned further."

The Malians who had encountered a guard on the other guarded caravel had the same experience—a sleeping drunk. When he was awakened and apprised of the situation, "Abadir" readily agreed to join the Malians.

The boarders on each of the captured caravels scanned the piers to make sure there was nobody on guard. Then silently, and very carefully, they untied the ships and raised anchor. That allowed the wind that was filling the sails to do what it had been unable to do while the ships were tied up—to move the ships slowly away from the piers. At that point, the sailors were able to steer the six captured ships and turn them about, facing the mouth of the harbor, and sail them out.

Once those ships were safely out of the harbor, they joined the three Malian caravels, dropped anchor and waited. Now it was time for the remaining two crew members on each pirogue to do their job. They quickly rowed their pirogues close to shore. Then they lit their fire pots and catapulted them onto the docks. As they did so, they kept an eye out for guards. Nobody ventured outside; everyone was no doubt inside the various buildings enjoying the festivities.

Once each dock was burning, the men turned the pirogues around and rowed out of the harbor to join the three Malian caravels and the six captured caravels. Then the three Malian caravels raised anchor and sailed into the harbor. They fired cannon balls at every building within range as they sailed around the circumference of the harbor. Before any defensive attack could be mounted, the caravels had exited the mouth of the harbor. Three men from each of the Malian caravels joined the six on each of the captured caravels to supplement their respective crews. Awolu and Abadir, the "captive" Malians who had been guarding two of the Portuguese caravels, were now questioned, released and assigned duties for the next stage of the voyage. The Malian crew determined that the sugar cane plantation Awolu had referred to was on the island of Madeira.

"Now, it's Spain's turn!" Hassan said to his crew on the Fatouma. He reminded his crew of the plan, "Our now-expanded fleet will sail far out into the Gulf of Cadiz to await the darkest part of night in two weeks. Then, onward to the harbor at Huelga!"

As planned, the now-supplemented fleet of nine caravels approached the Port of Huelga at midnight and dropped anchor in a semicircle offshore. Then the crews of the Malian caravels raised flags with Portuguese markings. The same six pirogues rowed silently into the harbor. There was no activity at all on shore or on the docks. This time, instead of attempting to board the ships at anchor, the men launched their firepots at the ships, at the docks and at the port buildings. Then the men quickly rowed the pirogues back out of the harbor to their own ships.

Once the pirogues were hoisted back onboard their respective caravels, they reported what they had accomplished—substantial damage to virtually every ship at anchor, to the docks and to the buildings. Hassan gave the order to raise anchor, sail closer to the harbor mouth, and await any ships seeking revenge.

They did not have to wait long. As each Spanish ship emerged from the harbor, it was fired upon by nine caravels. After two hours, the Malians could see at least half a dozen Spanish ships burning at the mouth of the harbor. Hassan gave the order, "We need not wait for more to attempt an exit from that fiery blockade. Onward to our next adventure!"

That adventure was to the island of Madeira. As they did when the fleet arrived at the two ports in Portugal and Spain, the fleet arrived at Madeira in the middle of the night. Six Malians boarded each of the two Portuguese caravels tied up in the harbor. This time, there was no one on either ship. Not far inland from the beach, there was a crude shack. Even further back from the beach was a somewhat larger dwelling. Suspecting that African slaves slept in the shack and Portuguese seamen in the larger dwelling, Awolu and several other Malians went ashore to inform the Africans of their choice to either join the Malian fleet or remain on the island. Not surprisingly, all eight chose to leave.

Pointing to the larger dwelling some distance away, Awolu asked one of the Africans, "Are they Africans or Portuguese?"

"They are Portuguese. They supervised our work." The worker

smiled, "They will be lonely and hungry living on this island by themselves and having nothing to eat but sugar cane!"

After that, the expanded fleet of 11 caravels prepared to continue sailing to the Canary Islands.

The Year 1460

Before the Malians had sailed from their Cabo Verde base, Khadijah had explained the next part of their plan. "Our goal is to destroy as much of the port structure and ships on the islands of La Palma, Tenerife and Gran Canaria, all of which are controlled by the Kingdom of Castille. We will approach the islands in that order and set fire to any ships at anchor. When finished we will keep sailing south along the coast of Africa and on to Cabo Verde.

"There is much fighting between the local inhabitants—who are the Guanche people—and the invading Spanish. We are told by Master Flamel that the next 20 years will be crucial for the Guanche, who face extermination or enslavement by the Spanish. If we can accomplish our goal, we can turn the tide against the Spanish."

Now, sailing away from Madeira, the crews changed the ships' flags again. They were relieved that the winds were in their favor and they made good speed. When they approached the Canary Islands, they hung back and waited for nightfall before proceeding any nearer.

As they had done before outside the harbor of Huelga, the 11 Malian ships arranged themselves in a semicircle before sailing any closer to the La Palma harbor. Once they were within firing range, they were surprised to see only three Spanish ships at anchor. Hassan said, "We can assume there won't be any slaves aboard; the Spanish haven't begun competing with the Portuguese slave trade quite yet."

Khadijah laughed and said to Hassan, "Then let's send these ships to the bottom!" On Hassan's signal, each of the Malian ships took aim at a Spanish ship and let loose with a barrage of cannon fire and flaming fire pots. They hit every ship and set it afire.

Hassan said, "What do you think? Do we need to go ashore and hunt down any of the survivors?"

Khadijah said, "I think we can leave them at the mercy of the Guanche." Hassan agreed, and gave the order for the Malian fleet to sail away, back out into the Atlantic to await another nightfall.

The next night at Tenerife, and the following night at Gran Canaria, the Malian fleet performed the same operation, and destroyed all the Spanish ships—four at Tenerife and five at Gran Canaria.

"Let's go home!" Hassan yelled to his crew on the Fatouma.

Khadijah said, "At least we've given the Guanche people a fighting chance against the Spanish. And we'll give them an even better chance once our Malian fleets begin patrolling these coasts and islands and destroying the ships of slavers!"

CHAPTER EIGHT

The Year 1463

During the months when the Malian fleet was busy destroying ships and ports in Portugal, Spain, Madeira and the Canaries, there was an ongoing ambitious development program in the Cabo Verde Islands pursued by Nicolas Flamel and Duke Keita. With the able and willing help of the newly released Portuguese crewmen from the late Captain Cadamosto's fleet, four of the islands were now developed with ports, housing and factories.

But recent reports from Malian ships patrolling the African coast and the islands to the west led Keita and Flamel to accelerate their plan to use the Azores as a base. "We'll have to send at least half our fleet of caravels to those islands if we want to stave off their colonization by Portugal." Keita looked concerned.

"Not half." Flamel continued, "In the last two years your patrols have captured six Portuguese caravels off the African coast. You could send those six, changing their markings to those of Spain. That would prevent Portugal from expanding its plan to use the islands to relieve pressure on their King."

"I don't understand. Are you suggesting the Portuguese king isn't that committed to developing those islands?"

"That's exactly right. He is promoting the colonization idea at home to counter the claim that his overseas developments only benefit the wealthy. And in the meantime, the reports of Spanish ships blocking access would further inflame the rivalry between the two countries. You can of course send more caravels as they become 'available,' not to mention the caravels you'll eventually be sending full of building materials and future citizens of the 'Federation of Mali and the Atlantic Nations.'"

The duke chuckled. "Who came up with that name? I'm guessing it was you."

"No, not at all. Yousef and his wife Maryam suggested it. You, of course, have the final say."

"Well, I have no objection. I like it. And I assume the idea would include not only the Azores and Cabo Verde, but also the Canaries and Madeira. Why not? We already have patrols there. And while we're at it, we'll of course need to get rid of those European names. Do Khadijah and Hassan have any ideas?"

"Why don't you convene a meeting with the ships' officers and draw up some sort of legal document?"

The Year 1466

The latest report from the Canary Area of the Malian-Atlantic Federation contained more good news than anyone had expected. "Your Lordship, the Guanche people, with the assistance of our ships posing as a Portuguese fleet, have finally defeated all the Spanish colonizers. They have extended their gratitude to us by presenting us full access to the ports built by the Spanish. And they have also handed over four of the six Spanish caravels we battled. They will keep one for their own use. The remaining caravel escaped and sailed south. The Spanish officers on the defeated caravels were killed. But some crewmen were Guanche slaves, and they reported that the caravel that escaped had a full crew and at least 20 enslaved Guanche people."

Keita looked up from the report presented by Sofia and Maryam. "Thank you. This is good news! Hopefully the escape of the single caravel would allow their crew to report to the Spanish king that the attack was by a Portuguese fleet."

"Perhaps, Your Lordship. That would no doubt further inflame the rivalry between the two would-be colonizers. On the other hand, should that escaped ship fail to return to Spain, the Spanish will have no reason to believe their new colony is no longer a Spanish possession. The Guanche people would be wise to prepare for more visits from the Spanish."

Keita turned the page of the report. "I see other good news coming, this time from the Azores. Our crews have successfully joined with the African slaves in overthrowing what passed for a 'government' there. But what did they do with the Portuguese settlers? The report doesn't say."

Maryam turned to Sofia, smiled, and turned back to the duke. "The settlers were actually relieved to be free of the avaricious local nobles the king had placed there as overlords. Before we could stop them, the settlers joined the Africans and killed the nobles. So, from the report we received, the Africans and the settlers have joined together in developing the islands."

Flamel added further good news. "Your Lordship, you'll recall that when our fleet captured the ships at anchor on the island of Madeira and rescued the African slaves, the Portuguese crews were left to either starve or make do with what food they could forage or hunt. Well, our reports tell us that the six Portuguese workers still alive on the island have petitioned for mercy. What is your recommendation? Should we take them prisoner or use them as laborers?"

"I think from what I have heard about the island and the Portuguese, their labor would be most useful to its development as another base or colony. So, send word to our ships patrolling there to assign those men something useful to do, such as planting food crops and raising farm animals. And of course, we must be vigilant in preventing further incursions from Portuguese ships."

The Year 1471

Lord Keita, on the advice of Flamel, decided on a 10-year plan to build and test a fleet of caravels. Once the fleet was declared seaworthy, the Malians would recruit crews and colonists to sail directly west across the Atlantic from the Cabo Verde Islands. Flamel had assured Keita that with favorable winds the fast caravels would make landfall in approximately five or six weeks, as long as the ships launched in the spring. "Your Lordship, the fleet will reach the north-eastern-most point of a very large continent, which, if we don't get there first, would be claimed by Portugal some 30 years from now. But of course, with the intermittent war between Portugal and Spain, I doubt either country will ever make that voyage across the Atlantic."

Khadijah smiled. "Your Lordship, I don't know who you had in mind for this voyage, but I'm afraid my ocean voyages must remain in the past. Hassan and I are 57. We and our two twelve-year-old twin daughters are looking forward to continuing our lives here as builders, farmers and fishermen. It's the same with Maryam and Yousef, who are each 53 and have nine-year-old twin sons. Sofia is 55 but has not decided whether she would want to remain here or make the voyage. I'm sure you can find many younger sailors and explorers eager to make that voyage."

Keita nodded. "Yes, I quite understand. Our community here needs you and the young people to continue to develop the islands." He turned to Flamel. "Nicolas, in the history you knew, what was the name of the spot on that continent where the Portuguese made landfall?"

"São Roque, on the northeast coast. In the history I knew,

Amerigo Vespucci, an Italian merchant sailing for Portugal, made landfall there in 1501 and gave the spot that name. But a Portuguese explorer named Cabral, on a voyage to India, inadvertently made landfall farther down the coast a year before that. He named the continent Brazil before continuing on his journey to India. São Roque is the location our fleet should make for. But we have less than 30 years to beat the Portuguese!"

"But you also told me that a few years before then a Spaniard completed a voyage across the Atlantic."

"Yes, in the history I knew, a Genovese admiral named Cristoforo Colombo, sailing for Spain, made that trip in 1492, and several more afterwards. But, as I said, Spain and Portugal are at war, so it is unlikely Admiral Colombo will enter the history books after all."

Keita frowned. "I'm confused. You traveled to our time from Paris in 1418. How is it you know what will happen in history 30 years from now?"

"You have forgotten what I told you before. From that time in Paris, I traveled first to 600 years in the past and then to 600 years in the future before I returned to this century. While I was exploring the future, I learned much that troubled me. I resolved that I should return to this century to attempt to destroy the ability of Portugal and Spain to embark on their disastrous campaigns of world-exploitation."

Keita set down the crude map of the Atlantic Flamel had given him. "So, our fleet lands at São Roque. What then? I cannot believe the land will be uninhabited. According to what you've told me about Cabral, he described the land as inhabited by people he called 'Indians,' thinking he had arrived in India."

"There are in fact many groups of indigenous people living all up and down the Brazilian coast. Many are related and speak some version of the 'Tupi' language. The group who will greet us at São Roque will be the Tabajara people. By all accounts the Tabajara people are friendly. At least they will not be hostile to Africans."

"How can you be so sure?"

Flamel smiled. "Think back to your own legends, Your Lordship. Your ancestor, Mansa Musa, is said to have sent a huge fleet across the Atlantic in search of a fabled land on the other side. But only one ship returned. Evidence unearthed in the future that I visited suggested some of those African ships did not sink, but actually made landfall and the sailors lived out their lives on that continent."

"So, you're suggesting we might encounter a less-than-hostile welcome, perhaps by people with some relation to us?"

"Well, at the very least, even if those legends are not true, we can be sure the Tabajara people will not attack us. Especially since we will be presenting them with many useful gifts."

Khadijah said, "I assume our purpose isn't to establish a colony of Africans, right?"

Keita said, "That's correct. Our purpose is to convince the people, not just the Tabajara but other groups all down the coast, that they must be prepared to defend their land against a possible threat from Europeans."

Maryam asked, "Why would the Tabajara believe a story of a threat they might face 30 years in the future?"

Flamel said, "Keita and I have been thinking that perhaps a few of the Tabajara would agree to pay a visit to the Cabo Verde Islands. We could show them how we've developed the islands, show them the Portuguese prisoners we captured a few months before, and explain how the Portuguese planned to expand slavery all over the world."

Khadijah said, "And in the meantime, what besides gifts would we provide the Tabajara and others?"

Keita said, "Things like ports that could be defended against invaders. And tools for building ships, housing and factories. Perhaps a school for instructing the people in those and other skills. Nicolas suggests we could even present them a gift of a caravel or two and instruct them how to sail and maintain them. And I'm thinking of asking one of the captains to consider hiring my two nieces on the crew as sailors. But I wouldn't want the other sailors to know that the women are related to me. I expect my nieces to be judged in terms of their abilities, not given preferential treatment. If they are known to be my nieces, others will get the wrong idea."

The Year 1481

"Captain Sofia, I see land ahead." Sofia Amina, captain of the `Oumou', walked to where First Mate Awolu was standing and looked out across the calm sea. She could see a broad grassy expanse of land in front of rolling hills. Awolu asked, "Shall I signal Captains Kareem and Khalil?"

"Yes, tell them to come up alongside us. I would like us to approach the land together."

As the three caravels drew closer to the shoreline, they saw a good-size bay with several buildings around it and set back from it. They could see docks and piers. Captain Sofia gave the order to drop anchor just outside the bay and had her order signaled to the other ships. "A few of us from the Oumou and the Kassa will go ashore in dinghies and see what we shall see. Captain Khalil will remain on board the Aissata with his crew until we are sure of our welcome. Lord Flamel has assured us the people will be friendly."

Two dinghies tied up to a dock. Sofia, Kareem, Awolu, Salman and three sailors got out and began walking toward the buildings.

When they stopped in front of the first building, they could see it was a type of dwelling. Kareem said to Salman, "Amazing! These buildings look like they could be from Mali!"

"Indeed, they could, young man." A wizened man of African appearance emerged from a building nearby.

Salman said, "How is it you speak our language?? And you look to be African as well!"

"That's because I am African. My name is Musa ibn Jabreel. My parents were part of the expedition sent across the Great Ocean by the great Mansa Musa more than 100 years ago. They were young children then. The expedition encountered many tragedies, and most of their boats sank. Only three boats survived to reach these shores. The survivors built these docks and buildings. As you can see, they built them out of young trees tied together with slender branches and long, tough grasses. They coated the roofs and sides with the thick clay common here. They had only small axes and shovels as tools. All their other tools and materials were lost when the other boats sank in the storm."

Kareem and the others looked around. Kareem turned back to the elderly man. "My apologies for our failure to introduce and explain ourselves. My name is Captain Kareem ibn Hamid, my ship is the Kassa, tied up outside the harbor. This is Captain Sofia Amina of the Oumou, tied up near the Kassa. These are our First Mates Salman and Awolu, and our sailors Jamal and Omar. The third ship tied up near the others is the Aissata, whose Captain is Khalil ibn Yousef. On our ships are 42 more Mates, sailors and workers, as well as many supplies and building materials."

"And what do you plan on doing here with your supplies and building materials? Are you lost, or is this an invasion?" Musa laughed at the question, and then started coughing. "Excuse me, but I need to remind myself never to laugh."

Sofia reached out her hand to shake Musa's. "No, this not an invasion. But our arrival is not accidental. We come with a proposal."

"Well, before you present your proposal, why don't we sit down under the trees and be comfortable. The sun will only get stronger."

The visitors followed Musa and sat underneath a huge tree with a fat trunk and widespread limbs. Salman exclaimed, "That looks like a tree we have in Africa. We call it 'albaobab.' Are they native here?"

"A similar tree grows here, but this one we brought here and transplanted. It is in fact an albaobab tree. Now, please allow me to change the subject. Before you present your proposal, answer me this. What kind of ships are those? I've never seen the like. Our original fleet consisted of several hundred large pirogues with sails."

Kareem smiled. "Our people still use pirogues, some very large, with sails, some small using only oars." Looking around, he said, "I see you have docks and piers but no pirogues. Have they been lost?"

"No, they are paying visits to our two other small communities farther down the coast. Now, tell me more about your ships. But before you tell me about your ships, let me just say how surprised I am to meet a female captain! Is it common in Mali for women to be in charge of ships?"

Sofia said, "No, it is not common at all. As far as I know, Sheikh Musa, I am the only one. Now, you asked about our ships at the entrance to your harbor. They are called caravels. They were developed some years ago by the Portuguese. These three used to belong to a small Portuguese fleet that attempted to attack us and were defeated. We learned to sail them and used them to attack Portuguese ports and shipping."

Musa looked puzzled. "And who are the Portuguese? Why would they seek to attack Malians?"

Sofia frowned and rubbed her head. "This is a complicated, sad, and infuriating tale. I know your people—that is to say, our people— have had dealings with the Arabs and Berbers who inhabit the northern part of Africa. And you may know that to the north of their country is a large sea that runs from east to west, from the land of the Greeks to this Great Ocean. North of that sea is a large continent populated by fair-skinned people. Some of them—the Portuguese and the Spanish—seek to dominate trade all over the world. One thing they have begun doing is buying or capturing people from the western shores of Africa, including Mali, our country, and Guinea. They hope to transport those slaves across the Great Ocean—this very ocean you once crossed—to this continent and use them in agriculture and mining. In so doing, they will encounter the native peoples and enslave or murder them as well."

"Before you continue, you must explain how you know this. Have these fair-skinned people already begun doing this?"

"Indeed, they have. It has been over 15 years since our people defeated that group of Portuguese, which took place on one of the islands in the Great Ocean. But before then, the Portuguese were raiding villages on our coasts and taking people as slaves. Even worse than that, some of our own people began raiding villages in the interior for slaves and selling them to the Portuguese."

Salman interjected, "Some of our crewmates on board these ships here were taken as slaves by the Portuguese. I was a slave myself. They raided our villages and put us to work on their ships."

Musa grimaced. "That is a terrible tale. Are these Portuguese still raiding your coasts?"

Sofia shook her head. "We have stopped them for now."

Musa looked out at the three caravels at anchor. "How could you stop them with only three of those ships? Surely the Portuguese have more ships than three."

Kareem smiled. "They had many more than three. But with these three caravels and others, we staged several attacks on their ship-building ports in Portugal and the neighboring country, Spain. After each attack we captured many of their caravels, destroyed many others, and liberated other slaves. We destroyed all the buildings, docks, piers and other ships in those two ports. Then, on our way back we did the same at several groups of islands that the Portuguese and Spanish were beginning to colonize. Since then, with an expanded 'navy,' we began regular patrols along the coasts of Africa."

As Musa contemplated what Kareem, Sofia and Salman had told him, a group of men and women emerged from the forest to the south of the beach. "Ah, family and friends have returned from hunting in the forest." The captains and sailors arose to greet the group. There were half a dozen men, three women, and four adolescent boys. Each pair of boys carried a deer, gutted and tied to two poles. The men and women carried spears and bows. They wore lightweight leather clothing and boots. The women appeared to be native, perhaps 30 to 35 years old. Three of the men appeared to African of the same age. The other three men were also African but appeared to be 10 years older. The boys looked to be mixed African and native and about 11 or 12 years old.

Musa spoke to the group. "I see you have had a successful hunt. I would like you to meet our guests, who just arrived in those ships at anchor." Turning to the sailors, Musa said, "Captains Sofia and Kareem, First Mates Salman and Awolu, and sailors Jamal and Omar, these are my family and friends. The three older men are my sons, Ahmad, Saeed and Kassay. Their wives have passed away from illness, as have the sons of Ahmad and Saeed. The younger men are Hameed, Mahmoud and Akil." Pointing to two of the women, Musa said, "These two are Kassay's daughter Soraya, married to Hameed, and Saeed's daughter Khadijah, married to Mahmoud. The woman standing next to the other women is Maryam. She was widowed when her husband, my son Mustafa, was killed by one of the large cats that are native to this area." Pointing to the two boys on the left, Musa said, "These two are Rafiq and Towfiq, twin sons of Soraya and Hameed." Pointing to the two boys to the right, he said, "These two here are Mowlana and Hassan, sons of Khadijah and Mahmoud."

Musa said to the boys, "Please take the deer into the cooking shed and then come back." Turning to the others he said, "Our guests have an interesting story to tell us."

After everyone was comfortably seated under the tree, Kareem spoke to the men and women who had just returned from hunting. "We have learned from Sheikh Musa of how your worthy community came to be here on this continent. He has confirmed that your community has its origins in our country, Mali, on the west coast of Africa. I, my colleagues here, and everyone on our three ships at anchor are also from Mali."

Kassay put his hands on his chest, bowed, and said, "Welcome to our country and our community. I think I speak for all of us here that we would like to learn more of your voyage."

Sofia smiled and also put her hands on her chest and bowed. She repeated what she and Kareem had told Musa. Then she said, "Thanks be to God that His believers are to be found on this continent as well as on the African continent. May I ask, does the community have a masjid? All of us are Muslim and we have not had the opportunity to pray in a masjid during the month we were at sea."

Soraya nodded and said, "Yes, we have a very nice masjid; it is behind those three buildings to our left." Indicating Musa, she smiled and said to Sofia, "Our venerable Sheikh Musa is the leader of our Muslim community and the one who designed the masjid." Musa smiled and nodded.

Kareem smiled in return and said to him with a sense of urgency, "My colleagues and I here, and those on board the three caravels, come to you with a very important request. The Portuguese and Spanish are relentless in their desire to conquer the world. They will stop at nothing. They will fight anyone who attempts to stop them— including each other! They truly hate each other, and our Malian navy has been exploiting their mutual hatred to cause them to attack one another. So far, we have managed to fool them into believing the ships that attacked their ports were ships from their enemies.

"We patrol the coasts of Africa, Portugal and Spain with ships we have taken from the Portuguese and Spanish. Our navy is quite large now—more than 70 caravels in addition to these three—but we are afraid that our navy is not large enough to prevent some of the Portuguese and Spanish to reach these shores. So . . . we have come to you in the hope of helping you create your own navy."

Silence. Then the boy Rafiq spoke up. With a sheepish look at his father, Hameed, he turned to Sofia. "How can we make enough ships like yours with material you have carried here?"

Musa frowned. "My noble captains and sailors, please forgive the boy. He often forgets himself."

Sofia smiled. "That is a very good question, Rafiq. Of course, our three ships do not carry enough wood to make an entire navy. We propose to make you a gift of two of these caravels, as well as the crew necessary to sail and maintain them. Myself and my crew on the Oumou, as well as Captain Kareem and his crew on the Kassa, would stay here to assist you to prepare to meet any invasion by the Portuguese. After our third caravel, the Aissata, unloads its cargo, it would return to Mali to assemble another small fleet that we would present to you in a few more months, with your consent of course.

"We are hoping you will be able to use the wood from your forests to construct as many other caravels as you need to be able to keep watch over your coasts. All other materials we have in our holds. We also have the necessary saws and tools of iron as well."

Maryam asked her, "And do you also have instructors who can teach us how to make such giant ships?"

"We do, my lady. On board two of those three caravels are skilled sailors and craftsmen with experience constructing and sailing ships of different types. In addition to constructing caravels, you will be able to construct pirogues such as the ones you see on our decks. Those sailors and craftsmen are eager to remain here with you and teach you to sail the ships and build others."

Awolu looked around at the group, and then at Sofia. "Might I ask a question of our noble hosts?"

Sofia nodded and looked at Musa. He smiled and said to Awolu, "Certainly. What is your question?"

"Do we have our hosts' permission to bring our ships closer to shore and have our crews and workers begin unloading our cargo?"

Musa turned to Kassay, who nodded. Musa turned to Awolu. "My son Kassay will direct the ships to the deep channel in our harbor. When you have docked, we will show you our warehouse for storing the building material. Also, next to that warehouse there is a building where our traveling crews live when they are home. Your crews may sleep there for now. When our own crews return in a few weeks, you may make room for yourselves in one of the other buildings." Turning to Rafiq he said, "Perhaps you and Mowlana could prepare the meat for the evening meal."

After the caravels had docked, Sofia introduced herself and the crews to the villagers. "I and my two sisters were once slaves of the Portuguese in their capital, Oporto. Since that time, we escaped slavery and returned to Mali, where we were born. My two sisters are currently living in the Cabo Verde Islands, east of here in the Great Ocean, not far from the African coast. There, a group of Malians are developing villages, ports and naval bases. I have decided to join this expedition and remain here."

Ahmad said, "How wonderful that you will remain with us. That is a wonderful bounty! But tell me, Captain Sofia, won't it be difficult to be separated from your sisters?"

"I suppose it will be, somewhat. But they are married with children. And very busy helping to organize the new towns being built on the islands we Malians have been developing." Sofia paused and noticed the sailors were ready to begin unloading the cargo. "Perhaps my officers and I should join our sailors at the dock to get them started."

As the sailors were unloading the cargo, Musa, Kassay and Maryam were escorting the captains around the village, starting with the building where the Malian crews and workers would be sleeping for the time being. Abadir was giving a tour of one of the caravels to the two boys Towfiq and Hassan. Ahmad and Saeed were talking to several of the shipwrights and carpenters about the types of trees in the forest. The Malians were relieved that there were a great many varieties of hardwood. One of the shipwrights, Dawood, said in response to Saeed's question, "We have brought a great quantity of pitch and tar out of fear we would not find it here."

Ahmad said, "That is wise, because although we know of several deposits of tar, they are quite a distance from here. And we have not developed a method for its efficient extraction."

Dawood smiled. "Fortunately, several of our experts on this voyage have learned how to extract tar. They learned that method from a European man named Nicolas Flamel. He is a very wise but strange man, from a distant country. He is not an African, but not Portuguese or Spanish either. He was born in a great city called Paris and has traveled the world over. Perhaps he will join us here when the next caravel arrives."

Ahmad said, "That is good to know. When a good time arises, we can show you the tar deposits, and you can demonstrate Mr. Flamel's method. I am sure I would like to meet this man, Nicolas Flamel."

As dusk deepened and the unloading had to pause, two boys came outside and announced that the evening meal was ready. The sailors and others from the ships eagerly followed the residents into the dining hall. The dining hall was of similar construction and size as the other buildings, built of young trees and branches tied together with long ropes woven of tough grasses. Thick clay was packed into the wood and grasses. Sofia could see that after long exposure to the hot sun, the clay had been baked into a waterproof surface. Three long tables were laden with various types of meat, including the meat from the two deer the hunters had brought in. Musa held up his hand to gain everyone's attention. "Before we sit, let us turn to the east and silently pray. Tomorrow we will show our guests the beautiful mosque we built soon after our arrival." Everyone did as they were bid, then sat down to eat.

Kareem, Sofia and Khalil were sitting with Musa and across from Soraya and Hameed. Kareem asked, "Sheikh Musa, you have said only three of your pirogues survived the ocean voyage. How many people were on those boats?"

"Our boats were the largest our people made. They had two sails and two sets of oars. There were 12 people on each. As I told you earlier, my parents were young children on one of the three pirogues that survived the passage. They told me stories of the angry Great Ocean, which did not seem to want them to complete the crossing. Indeed, the great majority of the ships were lost in the storms."

Khalil asked, "How many of the 36 passengers are still with you? You have 13 here."

"None of the original passengers are still living. As I told you earlier, my parents were among a small number of young children on board. I and the three men you have met, Ahmad, Saeed and Kassay, are sons of those young passengers. I am the oldest son. The others you see are grand children with Malian or native Tabajara parents. It is the same with the 15 men who are away on the three pirogues. The 50 men and women in the two communities they are visiting are native Tabajarans. So, you see, we are a small population. But growing and thriving. We are very happy here."

Kareem asked, "What about the other communities in this land? Our advisor, Nicolas Flamel, has told us of many peaceful communities all down these shores. Is that true?"

"As far as we know, that is true. We have visited several. We in our three communities strive to create healthy bonds with them. As you have heard, many of our people have married into the native communities nearby. We have built small schools in each of those communities besides the school in this village."

Musa took a drink from his cup. He looked puzzled. "Captain Kareem, tell me more about this Nicolas Flamel. Perhaps I misheard you, but it sounded like he had visited this coast."

Kareem was quiet for a moment before answering. "Captain Sofia here can tell you more about Master Flamel than anyone. She and her sisters were the first to learn about him when they were young girls living in Mali, before they were taken to Portugal as slaves. I will let her finish the tale."

Sofia smiled. "Thank you, Kareem." Turning to Musa she said, "Master Flamel is an older man, originally from the city called Paris, in the northern part of the continent called Europe. You have already heard of Portugal and Spain. Paris is in a country to the north of them." Sofia paused, took a sip, and continued. "Master Flamel is a genius and a scientist. He invented a time machine made from a common nautical device called a `spherical astrolabe.' Using that modified astrolabe, he traveled to the past and the future. When we saw him in Mali, he told us he had decided he would try to change the history he knew in his own time as well as the history he had observed in the distant future."

Musa said, "Again, perhaps I misheard you. Did you say that Flamel traveled to the past and future?"

"Yes, that is correct. That is what he said. Not only did he do that, but my sisters and I traveled to your time from a time 19 years from now using the same device, the spherical astrolabe modified by Flamel. It is a very long story."

Musa said, "And I am very fond of long stories. But before I ask you to tell me all of it, let me ask you this. Am I correct that Flamel visited these coasts in the past?" He chuckled and asked, "or in the future?"

"No, not personally. In the distant future to which he had traveled—600 years from now—he read many histories of these times we live in now, of the terrible wars of colonization and genocide carried out by the Portuguese and Spanish. He decided he would travel back to the past—to the time we are living in right now—and attempt to help the people of Mali destroy the navies of Portugal and Spain. We have been successful—so far."

Soraya's interest in this conversation grew when Sofia said that. "If I may join your conversation, how did Master Flamel help you destroy those navies? Is he the one who told you where they were located? And where is Master Flamel now? I don't mean to be rude."

Hameed said, "I have the same questions."

Sofia sighed. Taking one more sip from her cup she said, "Master Flamel is hard at work on the Cabo Verde Islands, off shore from Mali. You may have heard of those islands. By the time our little fleet here cast off from them, three of the islands were being developed with villages and ports."

Hameed frowned. "I have heard of them, yes. But I always thought they were just stories."

Sofia continued. "But true stories. My sisters and I brought with us several maps of the oceanic region to the west of Africa. Those maps showed the location of the Cabo Verde Islands, the Canary Islands and Madeira Island."

Hameed looked at Kareem. "You have seen those maps?"

"Yes, but only after our Malian brothers had concluded their raids on the ports in Portugal, Spain, the Canaries and Madeira."

Soraya asked, "And did you participate in those raids?"

"Yes. Khalil and I and seven other Malians had been slaves working on the Portuguese ships that landed at the first island in the Cabo Verde group. Sofia, her sisters and many other Malians were waiting for the Portuguese ships. They killed the three Portuguese captains, arrested the indentured Portuguese sailors, and freed all nine of the Malian slaves. It is a long story, but perhaps it is enough to say that it was Nicolas Flamel who informed the Malians where and when the three Portuguese ships would drop anchor. Those three Portuguese ships became the first caravels in the Malian Navy. You have met my First Mates on these caravels here. We liberated them during our raid on the Port of Lagos in Portugal."

Musa looked around and said, "It looks like we are the last diners still at table. If you don't mind, I would like to escort your group to the sleeping building." He stood and began walking out of the dining hall, the others following. Once outside, he indicated for the Malians to follow him.

CHAPTER NINE

The Year 1482

The remainder of 1481 had been very busy. The ships were unloaded of all cargo except for what the Aissata would need for its return to Cabo Verde. Kareem assembled a team to prepare to investigate the pool of tar that Ahmad had mentioned. When Ahmad was ready, he guided Dawood and another shipwright deep into the forest and showed them tar sands. Dawood said, "I think we'll be able to get a lot of tar from these sands. I'll have our extraction equipment brought here and we will begin the process."

Ahmad asked, "How is it done?"

"First, we insert a long hollow iron pipe into the pool of tar. We must transport a quantity of water here, heat it to boiling, and then pour the boiling water through the iron pipe into the pool of tar. As the water heats the tar it becomes more liquid and can be skimmed from the surface. I have seen it done in Mali, but haven't been directly involved." The men turned around and walked back to the village.

In the meantime, two shipwrights had been exploring the forest for trees suitable for building any additional caravels they would build. After they located enough, they brought a crew of men into the forest to begin cutting and dragging the trees into a large clearing where saws had been set up.

While the process of stripping the bark from the trees and sawing the trees into planks of different lengths and widths was underway, several men and women carried a long piece of hollow iron pipe to the tar pit. Others carried large tubs of water. Then a firepit was prepared, a fire was started, and the tubs of water were placed around the edge of the firepit. Once the fire was hot, one end of the pipe was heated and inserted deep into the tar. The other end was propped up on a log. Boiling water was poured through the pipe and into the tar. Several people were spaced along the edge of the pit with long-handled, flat-bladed wooden shovels, ready to begin pulling the softened tar to the edge of the pit. Other people transferred the soft tar into wooden tubs. Within several hours, they had filled a dozen tubs with tar. "This will do for now," said Dawood. "We will need to collect more tar when you have decided to build more ships. I have been on two teams of workers building caravels, and I am staying here with you for the next few years."

When Dawood and the others had returned, he explained that the process of building their first caravel would probably take more than three months. "Let me give you an idea of the first few steps. Preparing the keel would be the first job. Keels are made from single trees as long as 10 men laid head to toe. Carving up a tree bole to create a smooth, straight beam takes a lot of hard work and skill. First, the strongest of the men would use axes to hack out a rough beam shape. Then the surfaces are carefully shaped and smoothed using adzes. We learned to fabricate adzes with the help of Nicolas Flamel, and have included several in the cargo we have unloaded.

"When the keel is finished it must be lifted up onto a line of blocks. Then the men will hack out rough pieces from other large trees to fabricate the frames for the stern and the bow. Alongside the keel structure, men and women will assemble the floor and ribs out of smaller pieces of wood, then lift and attach that assembly onto the keel. Long flexible boards will be attached to the ribs."

Dawood stopped. "As I said before, I have worked on two ship-building teams. I will work with you should you decide to build more. Your community will learn much about caravels from the two we will leave with you. Once you have learned to sail them, repair them, and modify them, you might feel you should begin constructing others. I will help you do that if that's what you decide. I should caution you that if and when your shores are visited by Portuguese or Spanish ships, you must attack them with overwhelming force and firepower. They are merciless and you should show them no mercy. Therefore, my recommendation is that we start building another caravel or two when we have the necessary materials and training."

In early May, two pirogues were spotted returning from their visits to the other communities further south along the coast. Sofia was the first to see them as they approached the entrance to the bay. "Ahmad, do you think someone should row out to the group and reassure them we are not an invasion force?"

"Yes, that's a good idea. Perhaps I and two others should do that."

Sofia ordered one of the pirogues from her caravel lowered to the water. Ahmad, Hameed and Musa climbed in and rowed the boat out to the local pirogues. Musa stood and smiled. "Welcome back. I hope your mission was fruitful. I see one of the pirogues has remained down the coast, as well as the other 9 men. I hope they are well.

"Don't be alarmed by these ships you see in the bay. Some of our brethren from Africa have paid us a visit. They have offered to help strengthen our communities. Please, follow me into the bay and disembark."

In each of the pirogues there were two women and one man. One of the men stood and looked at Musa. "What assurance can you give us that we will not be deceived?"

Musa sat back down, and he and the others in his pirogue rowed it alongside the other pirogues. "If you like, I will join you, and my brethren will return without me. I will explain what has occurred, and when you are satisfied that our guests pose no threat to our communities, you may enter the bay and meet our guests."

After Musa had climbed into the local pirogue and answered more questions, the man he spoke to, Ibrahim, was relieved and signaled to the other boat to follow him into the bay and tie up. The boats rowed slowly into the bay. Before they reached the dock, the occupants stared nervously at the massive caravels and the Malian visitors assembled on the shore.

After the four women and two men had stepped out of the pirogues and tied them to the dock, Musa introduced them to the visitors. "Captains Sofia, Kareem and Khalil, these are our countrymen and countrywomen." Turning to Ibrahim, he said, "Please, why don't we move to the dining hall. You and the others must be very hungry indeed."

Ibrahim smiled, nodded, and looked at his companions. Turning back to Musa he said, "I see no objection, so let us eat!"

As Ibrahim and the others in the group walked to the dining hall, Sofia walked among the four women. "I see some of you are Malian and some are local people. My name is Sofia Amina. I am captain of the caravel Oumou tied up at the dock. The other two caravels are the Kassa, captained by Kareem ibn Hamid, and the Aissata, whose Captain is Khalil ibn Yousef. On our ships are 42 Mates, sailors and workers, in addition to the captains."

One of the Malian women smiled and introduced herself and the other three. "I am Fanta. I live here in this village. These three are Bintou, Fadimata and Iracema. They are from one of the villages one day's sail down the coast." She smiled sheepishly and continued in a low voice, "As you can see, they are very pretty and very young. I believe they are hoping to find husbands here; most of the men in their villages are married already."

Sofia looked surprised. Then she smiled and said, "Perhaps we can find someone here for you. If not from the original residents, perhaps from the sailors on our ships. They will be living here now among you. Anyway, I am pleased and honored to meet you. I look forward to learning more about your communities and answering questions. I am sure you have many, and have much to tell us about yourselves."

Before everyone entered the dining hall and took seats at the long tables, Fanta turned to Sofia and said, "I am excited to hear more about you, your home, and your ships."

As food was being brought to the tables, Musa made an announcement. "Our guests, visitors from Mali, will explain the purpose of their visit. But first, I believe everyone is hungry, so let's eat!"

The large dining hall became a festive place with much conversation, laughter and, of course, eating. Finally, Musa stood and looked around until the conversations died down. "Friends and family, a wonderful event has just taken place. God has blessed us, our village, and the villages further down the coast with people from across the Great Ocean, from Mali!" The people who had just arrived set down their food and drink and looked around at the Malians.

Sofia arose and smiled as she looked around. "Friends—my fellow captains, officers, sailors and I have come a long way and braved the Great Ocean to help you keep yourselves safe!" The diners waited for Sofia to continue. "In 29 years, unless the people on these coasts can stop them, several Portuguese ships will arrive. Their arrival will be accidental, as they will be on their way to the continent of India, a land far to the east of Africa. The Portuguese, as indeed all the people from their continent, like the Spanish, are unaware of this continent your people discovered when your elders were young children on ships that a storm tossed up onto these shores."

Turning to the newly arrived people, she explained what she and her colleagues had already explained to the other residents. After that, she continued, "So, what we propose is to help you learn to sail the ships you see tied up in your harbor and construct several more. `Caravels,' we call them. They were invented by the Portuguese decades ago, but we Malians have kept the Portuguese from using their ships from raiding our African shores for slaves, gold, ivory and many other valuable things. Myself, my sisters, and these Malian sailors you see here began our campaign against them by capturing three of their caravels on the islands near the Malian coast. Since then, we have attacked their ports and commandeered their ships. Our people now possess a formidable navy, more than 70 ships like these, with which we patrol the coasts of Africa and the islands nearby. We have set the Portuguese and Spanish upon each other by raiding their ports and shipping disguised as the navies of their enemies—one another!"

Sofia paused, smiled and said, "I am too old to talk this much." She turned to Khalil and asked him to continue.

He stood, bowed to the newcomers and said, "I am Khalil ibn Yousef, captain of the Aissata, the largest of the ships tied up in your harbor. My ship has brought building materials to you, including the most sophisticated tools and ship-building plans. After it is unloaded, and the cargo is replaced with food and water sufficient to make the voyage home, I and half of my crew will return to our home in Mali. The remainder of my crew—those skilled in carpentry and shipbuilding—will remain here to work with you. The other two ships are yours; we three captains and our leaders in Mali make a gift of them to you."

Ibrahim signaled to Khalil and asked to speak. Khalil nodded, and Ibrahim stood and spoke to the Malians. "I am sure you have already explained how you know what will happen in the future on these shores. I heard people at table earlier mention something about a 'time machine.' Could you perhaps repeat what you have already spoken of?"

Khalil said, "The best person to do that is my fellow captain, Sofia Amina."

Sofia stood and began speaking again. "My two sisters and I were taken as slaves by a Portuguese mariner and brought to the

Portuguese capital city, Oporto. We worked for him for five years. Then he 'loaned' us to the Catholic Church to work for a priest there. When the priest, Father Martim Rodrigo, learned that we were in fact slaves, and not just servants, he asked us to embark on a very special journey, a journey to 'correct history,' as he phrased it. He believed the practice of slavery to be a sin, and wanted to put an end to it. Indeed, he wanted to destroy the naval power of Portugal and Spain and prevent them from carrying out their colonial aspirations.

"He showed us something called a 'spherical astrolabe,' a nautical navigation device used by European ships to travel the seas. But his astrolabe had been modified by someone who transformed it into a machine capable of traveling through time, from the present to the past or the future. The person who had done that was Nicolas Flamel, a scientist who lived in the European city of Paris at the beginning of this century. Exactly how Father Rodrigo obtained the modified time machine is a long story, but I will just say that it had been damaged before the priest obtained it. He hired a Parisian master artisan to repair the machine. Once the machine was functional again, the priest helped my sisters and me to travel back in time to 26 years ago."

When Sofia said the words 'traveled back in time,' Iracema, the youngest of the newly arrived villagers, asked, "When did you begin your journey?"

Sofia chuckled and said, "My sisters and I used the machine 18 years from now. At the time we did that, the history of Africa and this continent was a tragic one—widespread exploitation and slavery instituted by the Portuguese and Spanish. Father Rodrigo's fervent hope was to have us go back in time to try and put a stop to that, to change history."

There were a few minutes of silence before everyone started talking at once. Finally, Musa asked Kareem to address the Portuguese threat. Kareem stood and said, "I am Captain Kareem ibn Hamid, captain of the Kassa. I and my crew will remain here with you to assist in whatever way we can. But our most important tasks will be to join you in building several more caravels and teaching you to sail them. We have become experienced in building caravels after having seized so many from the Portuguese and Spanish. Our shipwrights in Mali are at work day and night building them. Unless our Malian navy, which patrols off the coasts of Portugal, Spain and Africa, succeeds in intercepting and sinking the European ships that will otherwise arrive here in 29 years, your people will experience a good deal of suffering. We are hopeful that our forces off the Portuguese and African coasts will be able to keep that from happening. But Sofia has told us that in her time, two European navigators reached these shores. They did no harm here directly, but once they reported back to their monarchs what they had found, other European ships arrived. They began cutting down your forests and enslaving your people. We must stop that from happening."

Sofia added, "Not only must we stop them from reaching these shores. We also must stop a different group of Europeans from reaching the vast continent to the north of here. Twenty years from now, at least in the history I lived in before coming here, the Spanish monarchs will commission a small fleet of three ships to sail west to discover `India.' But as we learned, ships cannot reach India by sailing west. They would make landfall on Guanahani Island a year's sailing north of here."

Iracema looked puzzled. "Are you suggesting that we, the people here, must stop those Spanish ships?"

Sofia said, "Not necessarily. Our navy in Mali is attempting to stop that expedition from ever leaving port. We will continue plaguing the Portuguese and Spanish ports with destruction. We are hopeful we will succeed."

CHAPTER TEN

The Year 1484

The captains and crew were pleased at how eager the local people were to develop their capacity to defend against a possible invasion—including building more caravels. As hoped, they were able to finish one caravel in a little over three months. In addition to the ship-building operation, the men and women were also busy building more housing, another dining hall and another school. Harvest time began at the end of the month, and some of the grains, nuts, dried meat and dried fruits were collected and stored on the Aissata in preparation for its return to Mali. Khalil was particularly interested in the cassava root plant, and had agreed to collect a quantity to bring back to Mali to see if it could thrive there. Similarity of climate and the hardiness of the starchy, nutritious, delicious plant were big factors in his decision to import several boxes of the cassava plant.

Iracema was listening closely as Sofia, Kareem and Khalil discussed the impending departure of the Aissata for the voyage back to Mali. When they paused, she said, "I have a question. Would you allow me make the voyage with you? I'm very, very interested in learning more about Africa, having spent most of my life listening to the elders' stories."

Khalil looked at her as she stood her ground and looked at the captains without a hint of shyness. "What makes you think you could work on one of these ships as it crosses the Great Ocean? Have you any experience on a ship far out into the sea?"

Iracema said, "Not far out into the sea, no. But far enough to have experienced very rough, stormy waters. I'm also familiar with sealing leaks and raising, lowering, turning and mending sails."

Sofia and Kareem looked at her for a few moments and then turned to Khalil. Kareem said, "I think you should give her a chance, my friend. She'll be as safe as anyone on board. And there will be 14 or 15 other sailors, two of them women. Plenty of room, plenty of work. Give her a chance."

Sofia nodded her agreement, then asked Iracema, "But what about your family here? Do you plan on staying in Mali, or becoming a sailor? What do you envision?"

"My family are gone—no siblings, parents killed in the forest by animals. I'm alone. I wish to do something different. As I said, I want to learn more about Africa. And maybe I will decide to become a sailor. I am strong."

Khalil sighed. "Okay. Tell Abadir, my First Mate on the Aissata, to sign you up as a member of the crew. He will ask you what skills you have, and give you some tests to measure your physical strength. You will be assigned to work with the two other women sailors, and sleep in the same quarters. Now, let your companions here know before you report to the Aissata. Quickly! We depart at first light."

Despite experiencing two storms in as many months, Iracema was proud of herself. She had experienced nausea, of course, but during the calm periods she was not sickened by the motion of the waves themselves. She was also proud at how quickly she learned her tasks aboard the caravel, and especially how well she got along with the rest of the crew. The 14 male members of the crew were respectful of the women, and didn't complain that the women got to sleep in bunks on the lower deck. The men actually preferred to sleep in the open on the main deck.

Despite the length of the voyage across the Great Ocean, there was very little to do regarding the cargo; it had been securely tied down and hardly moved at all, even in storms. The sails, however, required constant attention. There was ample sail cloth stored in the hold, as well as two spare masts. Because caravels are very adept at sailing into the wind, the ship wasn't in any real danger of being becalmed mid-ocean.

Iracema was pleased to be considered a somewhat exotic creature among the crew. She was always being asked questions about growing up in the more remote areas of the coast. But when the crewmembers approached the subject of her family, she still found it difficult to talk about. "I never had any siblings, probably because my parents died when they were young."

Haniya, the older of the two sisters working on board as crew, said, "Oh, that's terrible. How did it happen?"

Now this is the hard part; I knew I would be asked this. "They were killed two years ago by large cats. I had begged them not to go so deeply into the forest in search of deer, but they persisted. Until they were killed. I actually heard the attack and ran toward the sound. But I was too late."

The sisters gasped. Bisma said, "I'm so sorry. To lose your parents is hard enough, but to lose them like that . . . that's much worse." She put her arms around Iracema. "You probably would have been killed if you had gotten there earlier."

After that conversation, the bond between the women grew stronger. Iracema was fascinated to hear about life in Mali, and asked lots of questions. Especially about the sisters' uncle, Duke Keita. Haniya cautioned her, however, not to talk about him in front of the other sailors. "We don't want them to think we were hired as crew just because of a family connection."

Bisma chuckled, "Even though that's exactly why we were hired. Only Captain Khalil knows our secret."

Iracema smiled and said, "You know, when we were all in the dining hall that first time and the three captains introduced themselves, Captain Sofia Amina said that in eight years, a Spanish fleet would make landfall at some islands a month's sail from the settlement. Do you remember her saying that?"

Haniya said, "Yes, I think she said the Spanish fleet would probably never leave Spain, because of the constant state of war between Spain and Portugal." Turning to her sister she asked, "Isn't that what she said?"

Bisma said, "Yeah. But it seems to me it would be difficult to make sure no Spanish ships left port. I mean, the battles between those two countries aren't incessant; as I understand it, they're intermittent. So, I guess it might be possible for that Spanish fleet to make the voyage."

Iracema frowned. "I think when I asked whether the Malian navy was contemplating stopping the Spanish, I must have been subconsciously hoping those islands would be protected in the same way my homeland is being protected—by the Malian navy."

Bisma looked at her sister and said, "What do you think, Haniya? Should we ask our uncle about the feasibility of beating the Spanish to those islands?"

Haniya thought for a moment, then said, "I think he would defer to that French guy, Nicolas Flamel, who seems to be the mastermind behind the successes of the Malian navy."

Iracema asked, "Who's Nicolas Flamel? I heard his name mentioned at the feast."

"Before you arrived with the others from the village down the coast, Captain Sofia told us a little about him. He's the man who invented the time machine you heard about. You'll meet him when we arrive in Mali or the Cabo Verde Islands. He was spending a lot of time on the islands, overseeing their development."

Captain Khalil expertly guided the caravel into the bay on Santiago Island, the most developed of the Cabo Verdes. Before the crew disembarked, First Mate Abadir announced, "The captain says we will only stay here two days to allow the dock workers to transfer some of our cargo to the warehouse and to take on more food and fresh water before we sail home to Mali. In the meantime, walk around, stretch, and get some good sleep tonight!"

As Iracema walked through the small town that had grown up around the port since the first Malians had arrived, she was startled to see an elderly fair-skinned man walking vigorously toward her. He smiled as he placed his hands on his chest and bowed. "Welcome to our first community of Malian colonists! I am so glad to meet you. I am Nicolas Flamel."

Iracema was speechless for a moment. "And I am very happy to meet you. I've heard so much about you, and about your time machine."

"Oh, it's not my time machine any longer. I gave it up long ago, 600 years from now." And when he said that, he chuckled. "Sorry. I really shouldn't laugh at my own jokes."

Iracema smiled, "But it isn't a joke, is it? I mean, the story that was told at the dining table in my country was that you converted a something called a `spherical astrolabe' into a time machine. You travelled to the future, and then left the machine there, in the future. But I'm not sure I heard correctly the rest of the story, like how you continued to travel in time without your machine."

Flamel was silent for a few moments, then reaching into his shirt he pulled out the amulet hanging around his neck. "I acquired this from the treasury of a famous Paris emperor in the year 1,000. It originally belonged to another emperor 100 years before then."

Iracema asked, "But didn't you use the astrolabe to travel to that time?"

Flamel smiled and said, "Oh, indeed I did. It was my first trip to the past. But once I used the machine again while wearing this amulet, I discovered I no longer needed the machine. So, at my next destination I left the machine behind."

"Are you saying the amulet is a time machine? How so?"

"As far as I can understand, the amulet contains something that `absorbed'—for lack of a better word—the power of the astrolabe I converted back in Paris. Now, to travel to any particular time and place, I need only envision that time and place, place my hands on this amulet, and it transports me there."

Iracema decided to bring up the subject of attempting to stop the Spanish from reaching the new world. "Master Flamel, I would like to make a suggestion, if I may."

"Certainly. Go ahead."

"At the dining table when I asked Captain Amina if the Malian navy was planning to confront any Spanish or Portuguese ships attempting to cross the Great Ocean, her reply implied it wouldn't be necessary, because blocking them from leaving their ports would be sufficient. Well, I worry that it might be very difficult to prevent those ships from escaping the blockade and crossing the sea. And if the ships do manage to do that, they would no doubt enslave or murder the local people. I would urge the Malian navy to protect those people, just as it is protecting my people."

Flamel raised his eyebrows and looked intently at Iracema. "I think your suggestion is an excellent one. I have considered that idea myself. But I do worry that the local people might not welcome ships full of Africans. Of course, our worries in that regard were groundless in the case of your people. But one never knows."

"Master Flamel, there is another part of my suggestion. I think the people on those islands are our people. Our traditions and myths speak of a vast migration of peoples from the north to the south on those continents. We believe we are related to them."

"Well, well! Your people's traditions are very accurate. You are indeed related to the people of the island of Guanahani, which is where the first ships of Spain dropped anchor in my time. In my travels and studies, my passion was to travel back to this time in an attempt to save the native peoples of that hemisphere from the genocide committed by the people from my land. Alas, it was not to be my task to do that. Other business prevented me. But not before I plotted a course from your land to the island where the so-called 'Great Admiral' landed. I provided that course to Sofia Amina in the hope that she or others would undertake the task."

"That is wonderful! I will certainly ask her about that. I believe that if it was decided to sail a group of caravel ships to that island, the crews should be composed of my people. Not only would our appearance mitigate the shock of seeing large ships coming to their shores, but the similarity of our appearance and languages would further ease any alarm on their part."

"You are a very persuasive advocate. When your ship resumes its voyage and reaches Mali, I advise you to speak to Duke Gbèré Keita. I believe he will be receptive to your idea. For one thing, he is concerned about the continuing threat posed by the Spanish and Portuguese. When you speak to him, tell him your idea has my blessing."

The Aissata left port at dawn of the third day. The voyage to the mouth of the Gambia River took almost four days. During that time, Iracema, Haniya and Bisma had decided to sleep on the deck to avoid the stuffiness and smells down below. Haniya said, "Let the men sleep below; it's our turn to enjoy the fresh air!"

Bisma frowned, "That's fine; I don't object. But there are only four bunks down there. Where do you suggest the other eight men should sleep?"

Haniya smiled, "Why, right next to you, of course. Don't be shy!"

Iracema laughed. "There's plenty of room on deck. We'll work out an arrangement."

When the Aissata came within two day's sail from the coast, they began to see the occasional armed Malian caravel. Khalil pointed out the distinctive flag. "Each of the ships in our navy flies the flag of our country. Except, of course, when we sail into Spain's harbor—then we fly Portugal's flag. And when we sail into Portugal's harbor, we fly Spain's flag!"

Iracema asked, "Captain Khalil, how big is our navy?"

"We are growing larger every month. When First Mate Abadir and I left on this voyage to the New World, our navy consisted of over 70 caravels. I look forward to learning of continued progress in our shipbuilding operations. Not to mention additional ships from our attacks on the enemies' ports and fleets."

CHAPTER ELEVEN

More and more Malian caravels could be seen as Khalil's crew sailed the Aissata toward the coast. It was nearing nightfall when the ship entered the harbor of the Malian city of Niumi. Khalil told the crew to unload the perishable goods quickly and leave the rest for the stevedores in the morning. "Tonight, you will find beds in the building next to the harbormaster's headquarters. Hurry now, get these perishables unloaded before dark!"

The next morning the sisters were pleased at the opportunity to show Iracema around the port. When Iracema said she didn't want to monopolize their time, they made it clear they valued the opportunity to do a little bragging—not only showing off their town but also showing off their exotic new friend from the 'New World,' as everyone started calling the continent on the other side of the Great Ocean. After a few hours of showing Iracema the port offices, residences, lumberyard and shipyard, they took her to the official residence of Duke Keita.

The duke's office was an impressive building attached to a mosque. Haniya and Bisma escorted Iracema into the office. Arash, the duke's secretary, looked up from a large desk and smiled. "Ah, the duke's intrepid nieces return from their voyage to the end of the world!"

Haniya said, "Actually, Master Arash, at present it is known as the New World."

Arash chuckled and said, "Well, are you going to introduce me to your friend, the Queen of the New World?"

Iracema's face went into a deep blush. Then she laughed. "Thank you, sire. But I am not queen yet. Just an ambassador from the peoples of the New World." She laughed again and said in a solemn tone, "My name is Iracema. I seek an audience with Duke Keita. I wish to discuss a very important matter with him." This time, there was no laughter.

Arash stood and said, "Please, follow me." He arose and walked into a hallway. At the end of the hall, he stopped at a large doorway, knocked and opened the door. He stepped halfway in and announced the duke's nieces and the `Queen of the New World.'

They heard laughter followed by a voice within the room that said, "Have them enter, Arash."

Arash opened the door wider and stepped aside. Haniya and Bisma walked into the room, greeted their uncle, and introduced Iracema. Bisma said, "Uncle, Iracema is from our little colony in the New World. She joined our return voyage so she could visit our beautiful Malian capital. She also comes with a very important proposal. We think it is worthy of your consideration. Our Captain Khalil and Master Nicolas Flamel also think it is a worthy proposal."

Keita smiled and said to Iracema, "Welcome to Niumi. Have you had a chance to explore our beautiful city?"

"Indeed, I have, Your Lordship. Your nieces are excellent guides! Niumi is a beautiful city. And I'm very impressed at the size of your shipyard and port. You are building caravels, is that right?"

"Yes, we are. With our shipbuilding crews of over 100 craftsmen, we are adding to our fleet of 80 caravels at the rate of one completed every 45 days."

"That's wonderful. I hope our people on the other side of the ocean can achieve that rate. When your nieces and I left my country on the ship Aissata, the workers had completed one caravel in 60 days, and were confident they would increase that rate as their skills improved."

The duke smiled and said, "That's good news. Our plan is that your people, including, of course, those of our people who settled there years ago, will gain the strength to prevent any attacks by the Portuguese or Spanish. Now, tell me about your proposal."

Iracema was quiet for a moment. "I first thought of my idea when I heard Captain Sofia Amina speak of a small naval fleet captained by Cristoforo Colombo of Spain. In Captain Amina's time in the future, Admiral Colombo's fleet sailed across the Great Ocean to a group of islands north of my country. If his fleet were to escape your Malian patrols, the Spanish would send the ships to an island called `Guanahani' 8 years from now."

Keita said, "Well, I think our naval forces will be able to prevent that from happening. At least that's what our commanders have told me."

"Yes, that is probably true. But only `probably' true. The Great Ocean is very, very large, as your nieces and I can attest. And despite the intermittent attacks on the Spanish and Portuguese ports by Malian forces, I think it likely that some ships could slip through. Lord Flamel and Captain Khalil agree with a suggestion I made to him."

Keita became pensive for a few moments, and then said, "Tell me what you suggest."

"My suggestion is that our forces—both Malian and New World—prepare to encounter the Spanish fleet not in the midst of the Great Ocean, or to try to prevent the fleet from escaping our surveillance. Our forces should wait for the Spanish ships where and when they will drop anchor in the New World—Guanahani—if they have been able to escape our blockade."

"But we have no idea where that island is! How would our navy find it in the vastness of the Great Ocean?"

"But my people know where the island is; or at least our ancestral traditions tell where the island is. Our people's traditions go back 25 generations. Those traditions say that our ancestors sailed from the Guanahani island group to our present home in a little more than three years. And the route was not complicated—they sailed south until they encountered land. From that first landfall they established their first communities. Then they gradually spread further and further south.

"What's more, according to Master Flamel, the geographic coordinates and the route are known. He has plotted them and provided them to Captain Amina should she ever decide to plan an expedition there."

"I take it your suggestion is that we sail north from where we have established a new community of African and local people and make an alliance with the Guanahani people; is that right?"

"Yes, but more precisely, I propose that three or four caravels carrying my people—that is to say, indigenous people—sail to that island as soon as may be practicable. The journey by caravel would of course be much faster than by the oar-equipped boats that my ancestors used."

"I see. In order to avoid any possibility of alarming the inhabitants, the visitors should look like them, not like Africans. But what then?"

"My lord, just as your Malian sailors approached my people with offers of assistance, my people would make the same offer to the Guanahani people. We would convince them of the need to prepare to defend themselves."

"But how would you convince them of a threat that might not appear for years, if ever?"

"Well, I think that the presence of a group of similar-looking people offering to build schools, houses, ports and ship-building facilities would be enough to assuage any fear that the newcomers had malevolent designs. The local people could either accept our offer or reject it. I think they would accept it whether or not they were convinced of a threat from the Spanish."

The duke sighed, then rose from his desk. "I can see the merit in your idea. By the way, when you return to your home, please inform Sofia that her sisters and their children are doing very well here. Khadijah and Maryam are getting on in years, of course, but they're still healthy.

"Shall we go down to the docks and see if we can find Captain Khalil ibn Yousef? By now he has probably received reports of the current state of our defenses, the size of our navy, our military actions against the Spanish and Portuguese ports, and our progress in developing the Cabo Verde Islands and the island of Madeira."

After leaving the duke's office, they heard the muezzin's call to prayer. Iracema asked if they might enter the mosque and pray before continuing on to their rendezvous with Captain Khalil. Keita said, "Yes, I think that's an excellent idea. I have been lax lately and haven't entered the mosque to pray. And I suspect you found praying on the good ship Aissata to be difficult."

When they entered the mosque, Iracema gasped at its beauty. "I had heard how beautiful your mosque is, but I hadn't imagined such beauty as this!" The four of them joined the other congregants, said their prayers, and left the mosque when they were finished.

As expected, Khalil was in the harbormaster's office going over bills of lading and shipbuilding progress reports. "Ah, Lord Keita. How nice of you to pay me a visit at the end of my journey! And my three excellent crewmembers, also." He smiled at Iracema and the duke's nieces and turned to Iracema. "I hope you are rested and enjoying our fair city." Turning back to Keita he said, "I must say, milord, you, the city fathers and the workers have turned Niumi into a model of progress."

"Thank you, Captain. And your crewmembers have given a glowing report of progress in our sister city across the Great Ocean.

In particular, Iracema here has presented me with an intriguing idea for enhancing the security of the New World against the threat posed by the Spanish and Portuguese. She says both you and Master Flamel think the idea has merit."

"It does, indeed have merit, milord. That is, if we are able to spare three caravels and crew them with enough trained indigenous people."

"I think it might be possible to spare three for such a mission. We have 80 in service so far and more are in the final stages of construction. Iracema tells me the colony in her country has built one caravel in 60 days and hopes to increase the speed. With the two we have given them they have three caravels already. What is your estimate of how many caravels we could spare for our next voyage to the New World? "

Khalil consulted the reports. "That would depend on how successful we are in maintaining or increasing our present number. I see from the reports here that recently there was a battle between two of our caravels and three Spanish caravels that attempted to leave their harbor. One of our caravels and two of the Spanish caravels were sunk. We saved our crew, and the survivors on the remaining Spanish caravel surrendered." Turning back to his reports, Khalil said, "Back to the question of our naval capacity, we have a minimum of 80 caravels. Do you think we could include three extra ships on our return to the New World, with the understanding that those three would become dedicated to the voyage to Guanahani?"

"Yes, I think so. They would be stocked with such things as lumber, iron tools, nails, wire, cannons, guns and other weapons. One of the new caravels would remain there, making an initial, permanent force of four caravels to assist in the defense of the people."

Khalil turned to Iracema. "While I was in your country working on the various projects, I was pleased to learn that many of the citizens were native people. I wonder how many would be willing to travel to Guanahani and remain to join the local people in preparing their defenses."

"Captain, there are more than 50 pure Tabajara people who consider themselves citizens of the Mali-Tabajara communities. Of course, all of us are quite happy living in these communities. But I wouldn't be surprised if we were able to recruit half of them for the mission to Guanahani."

Khalil nodded. "That would be wonderful, but not quite enough. Our experience with caravels has taught us that they should be crewed by not fewer than 11 men and women. So, at least 33 total."

Iracema thought for a moment, then replied, "We might be able to recruit that many pure Tabajara crewmembers. But keep in mind that many of our people of mixed Mali-Tabajara parentage do not look African at all. They would certainly pass as native in the eyes of the Guanahani people."

Khalil said to Keita, "Then what I think I should do, with your concurrence, is begin taking inventory of our stores, our fleet of available caravels, and personnel seeking adventure in the New World." Turning to Iracema, Khalil continued, "I assume from your comments that you would be interested in returning home to work on a plan for assembling a group of New World people seeking a new life in Guanahani. I would also point out that those people should be forewarned of the possibility of a violent encounter with Admiral Colombo and his crew. Lord Flamel has said that according to the historical records from his time there were more than 80 crew members on the three ships. In light of that possibility, are you still willing to organize and join a group of would-be colonists to Guanahani? "

"Absolutely willing, Captain. I look forward to it."

Khalil said, "Okay. I would have preferred that our ships wait until next spring to depart for the New World. But given the urgency of our mission, I think we should chance an earlier departure. We might encounter worse weather between now and spring, but perhaps not."

The five caravels were three weeks into the voyage across the Great Ocean when the first storm assailed the fleet. Iracema, who had been training at the helm with First Mate Abadir on and off during those weeks leading up to the storm, had her first serious doubts as to whether she really wanted to be captain—or even a sailor—any longer. When that storm had subsided, Khalil came up to her and patted her on the back. "You did pretty well, young lady. You'll be a fine captain when the time comes."

"Well, I'm not so sure at the moment. I need to lie down for a bit."

This particular caravel had been named "Arawaka," after the family of languages spoken by the coastal people. One of the other caravels was named "Taino," the specific language of the Guanahani people. On Iracema's suggestion, Khalil named the third caravel that would eventually sail to Guanahani "Tabajara," the name of Iracema's people. Iracema explained to her fellow officers that because of the close relation between her native language and the language of the Guanahani people, she felt confident she and her fellow potential colonists would have little trouble communicating. "Plus, Lord Flamel has told me that the people there are gentle, unsophisticated people. Better for us to arrive there before the dreaded Spanish!"

CHAPTER TWELVE

The Year 1485

It was mid-afternoon when the fleet approached the bay. Khalil was surprised to see six caravels, three tied up at each of two docks. "Six! The people have been busy! And they've built a second dock." Shielding his eyes from the sun, he said, "What's that name painted on the sides of the ships?"

Iracema squinted and read the name aloud, "'Quonambec'! That's amazing; it's a name sometimes used by nobles of my people."

Khalil pointed to the flags flying from the masts of the ships, "The colors are purple, yellow and green. Are those colors significant?"

"Yes, they are the colors of the `flame lily.' Perhaps you haven't seen them; they grow mainly in the forest, far inland from the coast."

"Well, well. It would seem the people have created a name and flag for their country!" There appeared to be no space at the docks for the five newly arrived caravels, so the crews dropped anchor in the bay. Each caravel had two pirogues lashed to the deck. Since each pirogue had a capacity of six, and each caravel had a crew of 12, the pirogues were able to transport all 60 crew members to shore in one trip.

Khalil and Iracema and the others were astounded by what they saw on land. Sofia and Kareem, assisted by their First Mates Awolu and Salman, had arranged a festive welcome for the Malian fleet. As they greeted and embraced Khalil and Iracema, Sofia said, "Welcome to Quonambec! We have made a lot of progress in your absence. Besides all the buildings, docks and ships you see, we formed a Quonambec Council. Mahmoud, Soraya and Musa are the newly elected members. Each council will serve for two years."

Iracema said, "I can hardly believe my eyes and ears! All these buildings and docks, an elected Council! And six caravels! Have you sailed them to see how seaworthy they are?"

Sofia laughed, "Yes, they have been sailed up and down the coast."

Kareem smiled. "Sofia and I personally sailed each one. They are very seaworthy!"

He paused and said, "Come, let's go inside and get you and your crew something to eat."

Sofia and Kareem escorted Iracema, Khalil and the rest of the crewmembers to the large dining hall set back at the edge of the forest. As they walked, the residents cheered them and welcomed them to "Quonambec." Iracema said, "I love the name you have chosen for our country." As she smiled and acknowledged the cheers and greetings of the townspeople, she turned to Sofia and said, "So many local people! When we left for Mali, there weren't even half this many indigenous people in the town. And before I forget, Duke Keita has asked me to let you know that your sisters and their children are doing very well; aging but doing well."

Sofia said, "I'm happy to hear that! I always think of them, and I wish they could join us here. Now, let me explain the changes you see here. Once we had completed our second caravel, we built our second dock and shipyard. Then we decided to launch a recruitment effort to hire more workers to help us speed up the shipbuilding process. Several groups of ambassadors sailed south along the coast to drum up interest. We were successful beyond our wildest hopes.

In a period of a few weeks, we recruited over 50 indigenous people from the villages, both men and women."

Iracema paused and then said, "That is very good news indeed! When I spoke with Master Flamel, I discussed with him my idea of having some of our indigenous people here make a voyage to the island where Admiral Colombo's ships would arrive should they ever escape the Malian blockade. He and Duke Keita both agreed that such an attempt should be made." She paused, and saw that Sofia was nodding in agreement. Then Iracema continued, "Not only did Master Flamel agree with the merits of that idea, he told me had once considered organizing such an attempt. He also told me he had provided you with geographic coordinates of the route from here to Guanahani Island."

Sofia smiled. "Yes, I do have those coordinates. More than that, I still have the spherical astrolabe my sisters and I used to come here. Besides being a time machine, it is an excellent nautical navigation device. Should you manage to put together a plan for such a journey, you must take the astrolabe with you."

When the group entered the dining hall, everyone who was seated rose and applauded the 60 members of the crew. The Malian sailors were stunned; even Iracema and Khalil were surprised at their reception. Kareem motioned for everyone to take a seat. Sofia turned to the crew members and said, "We have arranged the seating at the long tables so that you sailors can be interspersed among the residents. Please, find a seat wherever you like."

After everyone was seated, the servers began placing platters of meat and vegetables on the tables. Residents at each table made a point of serving the newcomers. Conversation subsided as the eating began. Finally, after more than an hour had passed, Kareem signaled to Musa, who then set down his cup and stood. The room became quiet as the people waited for Musa to say what he was going to say.

"Friends, this is a momentous occasion, as we can all acknowledge. Our brethren from across the Great Ocean have arrived with more help, both in materials and people. But I am told by our sister Iracema, sitting next to me, that a wonderful plan has been approved by the head of the Malian Federation. I know little about it, so I shall ask our sister to enlighten us." He turned to Iracema and gave her his hand as she stood.

She looked around at the room full of wonderful people, many of whom were her friends. Some were indigenous, some were Malian and some were mixed. She smiled at Khalil, who nodded and smiled back. Sofia looked at her with a question in her eyes and gestured for her to speak. Iracema cleared her throat and began speaking. "Friends and brethren, we all know what a wonderful bounty we are given by God. The Great Ocean has carried out God's plan for us. We have created a new nation, the nation that has now been named 'Quonambec.' We have joined together the peoples of Mali and the peoples of the New World in creating this nation. I was proud of us before I left on the voyage to Mother Africa, but I am even prouder as I see the wonderful flowering of our people!"

She paused to take a sip of water. Then she smiled. "I am sure you all have heard of the mysterious man from a place called Paris, a man named Nicolas Flamel. Our sister Sofia knows him well. Indeed, it was Flamel's time-travel invention that brought her and her two sisters to our world and our time—the spherical astrolabe. The history in which Master Flamel lived has been changed—not only by our sister Sofia and her two sisters, but by Master Flamel himself. God willing, the 'old history' will not come to pass. But we must do our part in carrying out God's plan. I learned from Master Flamel that despite all our successes in protecting the coasts of Africa from the scourge of Portugal and Spain, there is perhaps an even greater threat to our world.

"Our Malian Federation has enjoyed enormous success in setting those two countries against each other, almost preventing them from leaving their harbors and venturing out into the Great Ocean. I say 'almost' because on several occasions their ships have managed to escape our blockades. Not for long, however; our patrols on those occasions have destroyed or captured their ships."

She reached again for her glass, took a long drink, and resumed her talk. "I learned that in Flamel's history, 7 years from now, the Spanish monarchs would commission a small fleet of three ships to sail west across the Great Ocean in search of trade. I asked Flamel, Duke Keita, and the other leaders assembled in Mali what they thought of that history coming to pass. I suggested that it would be disastrous should that history become our history. I proposed that a small fleet be commissioned to prevent the Spanish fleet from reaching the island that the Spanish fleet reached in Flamel's history.

"Friends, I am happy to report that our leaders in Mali have agreed to commission such a fleet and set it on its way. And I am also happy to report that three of the five newly-arrived ships you see in the harbor are the ones chosen for that fleet."

When Iracema said this, it seemed that everyone started talking at once. Khalil rose and smiled at Iracema. She nodded and sat down. Khalil started speaking. "I was one of the captains who heard Iracema's proposal and I wholeheartedly agree with it. So do the other captains and Duke Keita himself. Iracema proposed that we send three of our ships on a voyage to the very island the Spanish ships reached in the future that Master Flamel warned us of—the island inhabited by the people of Guanahani. They are your brethren, cousins of the people who preceded you in reaching this New World more than 200 years ago. According to Flamel, they speak a variation of your language called `Taino.'"

As soon as Khalil said that, the questions started. An older woman rose and, pointing to two women sitting next to her, said, "My sisters and I are Tabajara people. When we were young girls, I remember my great grandmother speaking what I thought of as a `secret' language, one that she didn't want us to understand. I urged her, repeatedly, to teach my sisters and me and our closest friends that language so that we could keep secrets from our friends! Finally, I persuaded her. I'm proud to say my sisters and I haven't forgotten that language, although our great grandmother never told us the name of the language." When she said that, there was murmured encouragement throughout the room. She smiled and sat down.

Kareem smiled and stood. "Thank you. Maybe your great grandmother was in fact speaking something akin to Taino. Maybe there are others here who have had a similar exposure to that language." A number of people nodded.

Iracema stood again and said, "This brings me to my next point. I am hoping that there are enough indigenous people in this community who are willing to embark with me on a long voyage to Guanahani Island. However, I must ensure that everyone appreciates the risk. Master Flamel has said that the Spanish fleet that voyaged to the New World in his time contained some 80 sailors captained by Admiral Colombo. Imagine the difficulty and danger in attempting to protect an island of innocent, unsophisticated, indigenous people from the vicious, heartless, evil Spanish sailors in the employ of the Spanish monarchs!

"And yet, despite the difficulty, our task would not be impossible. The first thing we must do will be to make an alliance with the people of Guanahani Island. To do that, the crews on our fleet must be indigenous people. We must be able to learn the language of the people there— a language in the Arawaka family, perhaps similar to Tabajara. We propose to gather and train sufficient crewmembers from among the people in these coastal communities. We estimate we need three crews of at least 11 members each to sail the dedicated caravels to Guanahani Island."

When Iracema paused to look around the room, people began asking questions—"How long a voyage is it?"; "How difficult is it to sail a caravel far out in the ocean?"; "How long will our crew remain there?"; "What will they be doing there?"; "Wouldn't it be wiser to crew the caravels with more than 11 crewmembers?"; "What kind of weapons and tactics will our caravels use to block the Spanish from reaching the island?"

"Friends," she said to the assembled friends, "During dinner Captain Khalil and I had a wonderful opportunity to meet with our Quonambec Council members. We are very impressed with their wisdom and energy. I am hoping we will have several more meetings with them and with members of the larger community to discuss these very questions you have raised. For now, let us bring this wonderful convocation to a close so that our exhausted sailors and officers can find our way to warm beds!"

Late the next morning, very late the next morning, Kareem and Sofia showed up at the barracks where Khalil and the male sailors were still sleeping. Kareem informed them that a Council meeting would be held in two hours, at the conclusion of breakfast, which would be served soon. Sofia walked across to the barracks where Iracema and the female sailors were sleeping and made the same announcement. When she and Kareem began walking to the dining hall, they saw that they were being followed by Iracema, Khalil and the rest of the sailors.

As before, the Malian sailors were made welcome. Then Iracema announced at the conclusion of breakfast that all who wished to learn more about the plan to sail to Guanahani Island should assemble for an informational meeting in the Grand Mosque, followed by noon prayers.

Once again, Iracema was overwhelmed at the number of people who showed up for the meeting. She turned to Khalil and whispered, "There must be 75 or 80 people here!"

Khalil nodded. "More like 100!" The floor of the mosque was covered with people sitting on woven mats. Khalil turned to Iracema and said, "I suggest you walk to the lectern and start the meeting. Let me know when you want me to join you there."

Iracema walked carefully around the perimeter of the room to reach the lectern. When the conversations had subsided, she began. "I am very gratified to see so many of our people here, young, middle aged and elderly; women and men. Let me get started. First, there was a question about the distance to the island. Lord Flamel has said it would take an experienced crew about 200 days to sail there. But it should not be a difficult voyage; the sea is not terribly wild, at least not as wild as the Great Ocean. And during the first half of the voyage, we would be sailing close to the coasts, with many opportunities to sail into bays, drop anchor, and go ashore to search for fruits and hunt animals.

"We would need a minimum of 11 sailors to crew each ship, better to have 14 or 15. I am told that many of you have already learned the skills necessary to work as crewmembers on a caravel, and have sailed a short way out in the sea. And all of you, no doubt, possess the skills that would be needed to help the Guanahani people expand and fortify their communities.

"As I said earlier, in Master Flamel's history, the Spanish fleet captained by Admiral Colombo sailed from Spain 7 years from now. We must prevent that fleet from reaching its destination. We are hopeful, of course, that the Malian Navy will continue to be successful in blocking egress from the Spanish and Portuguese ports. But there is no guarantee that success will continue forever.

"As for the amount of time we will need to live among the Guanahani, we think we should plan on living with them that entire time, 7 years or more. We should help them to build strong, fortified communities. And we must provide them with the arms and building materials we have brought here on these very ships at anchor in the harbor."

Sofia, who was sitting near the "mihrab" at the front of the room, stood and signaled to Iracema that she wanted to speak. Iracema yielded the floor and Sofia said, "Dear friends, our sister has presented weighty issues for you to consider. I suggest we convene another meeting in a few weeks at this time, at which time certain decisions may be made." At that, people began speaking to one another and arising from their mats. Iracema walked over to Sofia, hugged her, and together they joined the others for noon prayers.

Throughout the rest of the month, Sofia, Iracema, Khalil and Kareem met with the Council—Mahmoud, Soraya and Musa—to talk about the status of the coastal communities. Toward the end of the last meeting, Iracema asked, "What I'm concerned about, among many other things, is whether taking 35 or 40 members away from their homes and work here to sail away into danger would harm the larger community here."

Kareem answered, "Well, I don't think so, and here's why. There are many men and women who showed their eagerness to join us here in Quonambec City to learn the skills involved in developing this community and building these ships and ports. Now that the ships are built and ports completed, some are eager to embark on another adventure. They are unmarried and healthy. I see no reason why they wouldn't welcome an opportunity such as you are presenting. In addition, most of the 60 Malian crew members who sailed with you here will remain here; only a dozen or so will act as crew on the caravel that will return to Mali. That will more than make up for the loss of 35 or 40 people who would join your voyage to Guanahani."

Iracema smiled. "I can't wait to see how eager they are after I explain what's involved."

The next few weeks were spent unloading the two ships that weren't going to be making the trip to Guanahani Island. The cargo was primarily iron tools and finished lumber that would be used in the various building projects in Quonambec City. The cargo on the three ships destined for the voyage to Guanahani Island was a mix of building material and construction tools. Those ships were also outfitted and supplied with a variety of weapons—cannons, catapults, lightweight swivel guns, supplies of lead ball shot and dozens of pots of flammable oil.

As the crews were busy inventorying and unloading the two ships that weren't going to Guanahani Island, Iracema was leading an informal tour of the three that were going. She was pleasantly surprised to see how many young, able-bodied men and women were examining the decks, holds, sails, weaponry, pirogues and cargo. As the time for the midday meeting approached, people from all over the settlement could be seen streaming toward the mosque.

The Council members brought the meeting to order. Musa smiled at everyone and said, "Friends, I'm sure everyone is as amazed and grateful as I am to see how our brethren in the Malian Federation have provisioned us so generously. Two ships full of supplies! And many of us have taken the opportunity to explore the three ships destined to make the voyage to Guanahani Island. Such planning!

"Now, we all know that a lot more planning will be needed before that voyage takes place. So, the Council, at the suggestion of Sofia, Kareem, Khalil and Iracema, has decided to devote the next 30 days or so to making sure all details are considered and plans formulated. During that time, let those of you who are contemplating signing on as crew weigh that decision carefully. We plan on having one or two more meetings during that time."

The first of several surprises occurred when three elderly women approached Iracema with a novel proposal. The woman who had spoken at the January meeting about her great grandmother's language said, "My name is Mayana. I and two of my sisters here, Ruburua and Macaney, would like to make a suggestion. Like you, we no longer have any attachments to Quonambec. Our husbands have died, and we never had any children. We would like to sign on as crew on the ships for the voyage to Guanahani."

Iracema was surprised. "But are you sure you could endure such a long ocean journey? It might take as long as a year, perhaps longer depending on the sea and how often we would need to reprovision our stocks. What specific skills do you possess? There is limited space on a caravel. We plan on having a crew of no more than 15 on each ship."

Ruburua said, "During the meeting, my sister Mayana commented on our familiarity with the Taino language, which we learned as children. If that language is indeed similar to the language spoken by the people of Guanahani Island, then your crewmembers would need to have some familiarity with it at the outset. My sisters and I could teach the crewmembers during the voyage!"

Iracema said, "Certainly, it would be helpful if our crews were able to communicate with the local people. However, you haven't answered my other question. What experience do you have on a seagoing ship?"

Macaney smiled. "Not much, it is true. But some. We went out several times on the caravels when they were sailed down the coast to approach people who might want to work here in the port. We were not afflicted with seasickness, and we proved we could do a long day's work on board just as any well as a younger person."

Sofia walked over to speak to Iracema and saw her speaking to the three elder women. She greeted them, and as Iracema summarized what the women were requesting, Sofia listened carefully. Then she said, "The decision is yours, Iracema. I have no objection, and their proposal would seem to be a good idea." Turning to the women, she said, "I have seen your work here at the village and on the ships. You are strong, intelligent workers. But give your proposal more thought. Keep in mind that the voyage might be challenging—rough seas at times, cramped quarters, little privacy, poor food. Also keep in mind that in all likelihood you would not be returning to your homeland here."

The other surprise that occurred was the number of people expressing their interest in signing up as crew for the voyage. Many of them were middle aged men and women interested in a new life. Others were young people with a sense of adventure. Each of them already had an introduction to sailing a caravel. When Iracema interviewed each of them, she made sure to point out that life on the island might be difficult, and there might be armed clashes with the Spanish ships captained by Colombo.

She decided to call a general meeting with those she had interviewed and who still wished to sign up. In the meeting, she said, "I am deeply gratified, relieved and honored by your willingness to join me and my officers as crew members. Before we make our decision, please make sure you have taken care of all your responsibilities to your community here. We will do the same—it is important that we not leave this community short-handed. Also, those of you who are selected will be the most able-bodied sailors.

"We have already selected the captains of the other two ships, as well as the First Mates of all three ships. My First Mate will be Caua, a mature woman of strong mind and body. The captains of the other two ships will be Janaina, a young woman with a lot of experience handling boats all up and down the coast, and Ruda, a strong older man with excellent navigation skills. Moacir and Ubirajara, two strong younger men, are their First Mates. To help you gain a bit more experience, the First Mates will work with groups of those who wish to apply. They will take groups of 10 on board each ship and provide some instruction and testing. We hope to make our decision in the next few months."

The Year 1486

The three Guanahani-bound caravels were declared seaworthy after a thorough inspection for cracks and other damage. By the end of the month, they were ready to be stocked with barrels of water, dried meat, ship's biscuit, roasted grains, and fresh and dried fruits.

They had already been loaded with lumber, nails, sailcloth, tar and anchors that they anticipated using on the island to build at least one caravel and several pirogues. They also had two crates of weapons that would be needed to arm the new ships they would build.

Each ship was now ready with a crew of 15. Iracema assembled all three ships' crews at the main dock and went over the plan for the voyage. "You have all gone through a thorough training on the ships. You know your jobs. The voyage will take at least 250 days, probably more should there be more severe storms than is normal on these coasts. Other delays might occur during the search for sources of fresh water, fish and fruits in the various bays where we will stop along the way. The captains, in consultations with Sofia regarding information from Master Flamel, expect to find such bays and inlets every week or two.

"During the first half of the voyage, we will be sailing not far out in the open sea, following the curvature of the coastline. Then, when the coastline has curved sharply to the west, our route will be more or less straight north. That route will bring us past several groups of islands before we reach our destination—Guanahani Island. We will of course, by necessity, drop anchor several times offshore of those islands in order to replenish our stocks of water, fish and fruit. But we must beware of contact with any local people we meet. Some may be hostile, so our landing parties must be armed and cautious. And another thing, a very important thing. We will all be students— language students—being taught by our elder sisters, Macaney, Ruburua and Mayana. We believe—hope, actually—that the people of Guanahani Island speak a language very closely akin to Taino, a language these sisters were taught by their great grandmother when they were young."

The ships began their voyage and were blessed with fair weather and calm seas as they sailed close to the coastline. When Iracema calculated that the voyage was half completed, it was time for the ships to leave the coastline and begin sailing north. Using the astrolabe, she was able to plot a route to Guanahani Island at 24 degrees latitude by 74 degrees longitude. Following the route Flamel had advised, they sailed northwest for more than a month and passed numerous islands, apparently uninhabited, where they were able to obtain fresh water, fruits and fish.

When they had almost passed a very large island, Iracema signaled a change to sail due north. After three weeks they passed through a group of small islands where they once again were able to obtain water, fruits and fish. As they approached a small island just north of 22 degrees latitude by 73 degrees longitude, Iracema gambled that it would be uninhabited. Using the mirrored lantern, she signaled for the other ships to follow her into a small bay, where they dropped anchor. All 45 crewmembers looked out across the clear, shallow water, and could see no signs of human habitation. One by one, sailors began jumping off into the warm water. They enjoyed swimming in the bay before heading onto shore to get some walking exercise.

"This appears to be uninhabited, but I do not think we should linger long. Fill a few water barrels from these streams and float them back to the ships. Then we should raise anchor and continue on our way. We have about another two months to go!" Iracema wasn't worried about being attacked by humans on that island, but felt there was no reason to linger ashore any longer.

The time passed very slowly, and the crews were tired of being on board a ship. Soon, a crew member shouted from the top of the mast that she had sighted an island. Iracema checked the coordinates with the astrolabe and determined the island had to be Guanahani Island. She signaled to the other ships to follow her to the southern end of Guanahani Island, and to drop anchor outside the mouth of a bay. Once the three ships were safely anchored, she signaled for the other two captains to join her aboard her caravel. When they had rowed to her ship and joined her, she explained her plan. "According to Master Flamel, this island will be the first land that Admiral Colombo will sight and explore. Although in Flamel's history Admiral Colombo reported the people to be simple and friendly, we should nonetheless be on our guard against treachery or violence. We will go ashore in these boats."

CHAPTER THIRTEEN

When the boats reached the shore, the captains got out and hauled them onto the beach. They were surprised to see several dozen men, women and children gathered nearby. Iracema and the two other captains turned to face them, gestured a greeting and began walking toward them. Two elderly people, a large man and a large woman, stood apart from the rest of the people, arms crossed, and waited silently as the three captains approached. Iracema smiled at them and said in halting Taino, "Greetings from Quonambec! We are your brethren from the Southern Continent. I am Captain Iracema and these are Captains Janaina and Ruda. We are captains of these three ships you see in your harbor."

The woman uncrossed her arms and spoke. "Welcome to our land. I am called Grandmother Bakutu. I am pleased to hear you speak our language so well. How did you learn it?"

Ruda smiled. "Thank you for your compliment. But we feel our ability is very childlike. We are learning, and wish to learn more. Why are you called `grandmother'?"

Bakutu smiled, "Well, that is a very long story."

The man standing next to Bakutu said to Iracema, "It is true; you speak our language well. My name is Hiriko, `generous', also a very long story." Then he chuckled. "Most of our names have very long stories."

Bakutu looked out at the three ships at anchor. "Are there more people on your ships? Do you think they would like come ashore?

Our people are preparing a feast to celebrate the end of the harvest. I would like to invite you to join us."

Iracema sighed a sigh of relief. "I will signal to the crews on our ships and convey your most generous invitation."

After Iracema had done that, Bakutu said, "You come from the Southern Continent. I and everyone here would like to learn more about that place and your voyage here. I would also like to know more about your ships. We have never seen the like. You see our boats pulled up on land. They are primitive in comparison. But enough questions for now. When the rest of your crew comes ashore, let us go to the village."

The walk to the village did not take long. With Bakutu leading, Iracema by her side, the group walked together along a wide path with fields of sugar cane, beans and maize on either side. Hiriko had asked that they walk in pairs, a resident alongside a crew member.

At first the crew members were hesitant to initiate conversation because of their fear that the Taino language would be too different from their Tabajara language. But the sailors soon found that Taino bore a very close resemblance to Tabajara. As their conversations progressed, they lost all hesitancy.

When they emerged from the fields of crops, they saw in front of them a ring of small buildings made of immature trees tied together in bundles in the shape of overturned baskets. Windows had been cut in the sides, and the tops were open to allow smoke from cook fires to escape. Here and there were small coops of ducks, turkeys, peccaries and small deer. They also saw, and smelled, racks of large fish being dried and smoked.

There was a large open-sided building in the middle of everything. Bakutu gestured to it and said, "Please join us for our harvest feast."

Iracema looked surprised. "Our people also celebrate the harvest feast. I have to admit, we have lost track of the time, being on board ships for most of the past year."

Bakutu said, "I can imagine how difficult it must have been to observe the time of the year when sailing from the Southern Continent. You say the voyage took most of a year. Many of our people have travelled throughout this watery region full of islands small and large. But most of us have never seen what you call the Southern Continent. I say most, but there is one person who might know of that land—our beloved 'Hatsu,' the First Born. You will meet her at the Feast. Come, let us gather your crew together and make our entrance to the Grand Hall."

With the three captains escorted by Bakutu and Hiriko, and each of the sailors escorted by a village member, they entered the Hall and were greeted by the rest of the village. The villagers, captains and sailors sat together on long tables on the sides of the Hall. Hiriko and Bakutu took seats at the table in front facing out at the rest of the diners. There was an empty seat in the middle of that table, apparently reserved for someone important. The smell of roasted meat and maize permeated the air. Soon, servers brought out large trays of food and placed them on a large table in the middle of the room. Other servers placed earthenware jugs of water on each table. Earthenware platters were placed in front of the diners, along with utensils of hardwood.

Hiriko stood and addressed the people, "Welcome to our guests from the Southern Continent! And now let us all stand and welcome our beloved Hatsu!" Everyone stood and waited. Then a very elderly woman, escorted by two large women, entered the Hall. She smiled as she turned this way and that, seemingly acknowledging everyone personally. When she reached her place of honor at the front table, she gazed at the guests and said, "Welcome to you all. I am full of joy to be able to meet my distant kindred from that far-away land I once visited as a child. But there will be time for talk later. Now it is time for us to celebrate and honor our beloved home, 'Lu'um,' our Earth!" She signaled to Hiriko, lowered her gaze, and began chanting. Hiriko did the same, followed by everyone else. Iracema whispered to

Bakutu, "That is a beautiful chant," and then joined in. Hatsu stopped, hummed a short syllable, and sat down. With that everyone else sat down.

The servers standing next to the table holding the platters of food began cutting the meat. They placed the pieces, along with the ears of maize, on platters that they distributed around the room. The sailors, at first hesitant to begin eating, were soon persuaded by the aroma of the meat and maize to give in to their famished appetites. They were not alone.

Hiriko stood after a respectful amount of time had passed and everyone seemed to be ready to hear the sailors' story. "Friends, I would like to introduce the three captains of this fleet that has paid us a visit from the Southern Continent—Captain Iracema, Captain Janaina and Captain Ruda." Turning to the captains, Hiriko said, "Now, which one of you would like to speak?"

Iracema smiled, stood, and faced the audience. "Please forgive my poor command of your language. Although I cannot fault our teachers. They are sailors like us, and their duties on board often left them little time for instruction."

Hatsu looked at her, smiled, and said, "Nonsense! You speak it beautifully. Even I, an elderly woman who has celebrated more than 100 revolutions around the sun, can understand you perfectly. Please continue and forgive my interruption."

"You are too kind. I must say that we all feel relieved at the similarity of Taino to our native language of Tabajara. We hope that as a result our communication with you will not suffer any misunderstandings. But before I explain the purpose of our voyage to your land, let me introduce our teachers. Please welcome Macaney, Ruburua and Mayana. They learned Taino as children from their great grandmothers." The three women stood and smiled as their hosts applauded.

Iracema waited for them to take their seats before continuing.

"Friends, our arrival to this wonderful island was no accident of poor navigation or wayward ocean currents. We were told of your existence by a wonderful man from a large continent to our east, across the Great Ocean. His name is Nicolas Flamel, from a city called Paris on the northern part of that continent. We consider him a historian and world traveler.

"But before I tell you his story, let me tell you more about my home and home of all of us captains and sailors—the Southern Continent. I have learned that your beloved matriarch, Hatsu, has visited that continent, and perhaps remembers it. It lies a year's journey to the south; a year if sailing in one of our ships, called `caravels.' But much longer if attempted in a smaller craft such as yours and the ones called `pirogues' that we carry on board our caravels.

"That continent, which we call `Quonambec," is a vast land stretching to the bottom of our globe and almost as far to the west. It is home to many peoples, kindred to us all. Our teacher, Master Flamel, has taught us much of their history—when and from where they traveled to that continent. For, you see, those people—your people and our people—migrated there from the far north on our globe hundreds of years ago.

"But that is a long story that I need not go into yet. For now, I need to bring the most important topic into focus—the threat you and perhaps other people in these islands face from a menace that will come here from across the Great Ocean in about 6 years. Our people first learned of this threat 40 years ago when a fleet of three caravels dropped anchor at an island in the middle of the Great Ocean. The captains of those caravels were from that land across the Great Ocean. The captains had been ordered by their sovereign, the king of a country called Portugal, to sail to a vast continent to their south called `Africa' and kidnap people to work as slaves. Their fleet was blown off course and instead of landing on the coast of Africa, they landed on an island in the middle of the Great Ocean.

"Now, this is one of the mysteries of my story. Those Portuguese captains were captured and killed by people waiting for the ships—people who had learned, beforehand, the exact date of their arrival. The crewmen on those captured caravels had been taken as slaves from Africa, and were relieved at this turn of events. They joined the people who had liberated them. They taught their liberators how to sail the caravels and, eventually, how to build more of them.

"I will shorten my story because my throat is getting dry and your minds are filling up with questions. The liberators had arrived on that island from an African empire called Mali. They returned to Mali and convinced the ruler to build a fleet to sail to the Southern Continent. Now before I go any further, I'll answer your questions. That will be more efficient perhaps."

There was a short period of silence before Hatsu signaled for assistance in getting to her feet. Then she smiled and said, "I'm sure I'm the only person here who has heard about the land called Mali. My grandmother had been a two-year-old child in one of the groups that the great Mali king Mansa Musa commissioned to sail across the Great Ocean 140 years ago. Their boat, a pirogue similar to the ones on board your ships, became separated from the rest of the fleet and was shipwrecked on an island not far to the south of here. My grandmother grew up on that island, married a local man and had one child, my mother. She married a local man and they had one child 100 years ago, me.

"My mother told me that her mother's people had come from a land called Mali, a land far away across the Great Ocean. Her mother said she had been told it was a great empire ruled by Mansa Musa, and the people followed a glorious religion. But she didn't know much more than that because she was only a child during the voyage.

"My father taught me to sail, and for years I explored these islands. I eventually settled here. I would very much like to learn more about the rest of that fleet." With that she sat back down and waited for her answer.

Iracema, the other captains, and the crews as well, were shocked at what Hatsu had said. Finally, Iracema spoke. "This is stunning news. Another connection to Africa! I find it ironic that when the Quonambec Council put together their plan to send me, my fellow captains and crewmembers here, they decided not to include any Malians in the crew for fear that Black people would alarm the inhabitants here! Instead, they chose indigenous people exclusively."

For the next few moments there was silence. Then people started asking to speak. One middle aged woman said, "My name is Siba. I am one of those who have sailed these islands quite extensively and in so doing have collected many tales of our history. But like our esteemed Hatsu, I never learned much about the lands across the Great Ocean. I would like to hear more of those lands, but even more would I like to learn more about this mysterious man you call Nicolas Flamel and the place he came from, Paris."

Iracema said, "I would like Captain Ruda to speak about Master Flamel, since I am feeling tired and, to be honest, unsure of where to begin."

With that, Captain Ruda arose and gazed out at the people in the Hall. "I pride myself for being an expert navigator, but even I could not have guided my ship here without the benefit of an advanced mariner's device called a `spherical astrolabe.' Captain Iracema has a very advanced spherical astrolabe, one that not only guided us here by following the stars, but which was modified by Master Flamel himself. Flamel was born in and grew up in that city called Paris. He was notorious, you might say, because he dabbled in a mysterious subject known as `alchemy,' a branch of science looked down upon by other scientists. Flamel obtained a common spherical astrolabe, took it apart, and modified it to be capable not only of navigating the world's oceans, but navigating what he called the `interstices of time itself.'"

Ruda took a drink of water and waited for the first question. He had hardly swallowed his water when a young man stood and said,

"Please explain how one navigates time, other than in the usual way, from the past to the future."

Ruda smiled. "That is almost exactly what Flamel was asked. The Master explained that after creating his modified astrolabe, he used it to transport himself back and forth through time. Then he made an auspicious voyage 600 years into the future. When he saw how our world in the future had been savaged and exploited mercilessly by the leaders, pirates and plunderers of Europe, most especially by mariners from Portugal and Spain, Master Flamel traveled back to our time to try to assist us in blocking the Europeans from exploiting Africa and the Southern Continent."

When Ruda said that, several people spoke at once. He pointed to one elderly man and invited him to ask his question. The man said, "My name is Guaitiao. I have never heard of traveling from the past to the future except in the usual way, from one day to the next. But what I want to hear more about is the place you come from, Quonambec. And Mali as well."

Several people said, almost simultaneously, "Wait. Tell us about the threat you say we're facing in six years. Who are they and where will they come from?"

Janaina arose, looked at Iracema, and addressed the people. "I can summarize the history that Master Flamel studied. A very skillful European navigator and ship captain known as Cristoforo Colombo assembled a fleet of three ships like ours and a crew of 80 men. With orders from the monarchs of Spain, he sailed west from Europe hoping to arrive at a land known as 'India.' But he didn't know that India lay on the other side of the globe. Instead, he arrived here. Precisely here. This Colombo man is an evil mercenary, murderer, exploiter and ruthless savage. In the history that Nicolas Flamel taught us, Colombo had no mercy or respect for other people. He would take advantage of the people on this island, and return again and again here and to the other islands in this region. He would seize people and make them slaves, just like the Portuguese are attempting right now off the coasts of Africa. Our mission here is to stop Colombo, and we think we can do that with your help."

Janaina stopped to take a drink of water. Before she continued, Bakutu rose and signaled she would like to speak. Janaina nodded and sat down. Bakutu frowned and said, "If I heard you correctly, you say these 80 merciless men from Europe will come here to exploit and enslave us. And you hope to prevent them from doing that. But you have fewer than 50 sailors. I'm afraid that being so outnumbered would make it difficult to stop the Europeans should you attempt to confront them head on."

She looked around the room, smiled, and continued, "But your chances of victory would perhaps be better if you took advantage of the element of surprise and were able to hide your ships from view." She chuckled and then addressed the crowd, "Now, I think several of you can read my mind. Would someone like to elaborate on the element of surprise?"

Siba stood up again and said, "Our little island has numerous lakes. It has two bays. But a ship approaching from the east will at first only see one bay, the mouth of which faces east. After the ship sails to the middle of that bay, however, a smaller bay becomes visible that opens out to the south. That opening is very narrow, barely wide enough for a ship such as yours to pass through. But once a ship enters that bay, the bay bends sharply to the left after a short distance and then expands. The bend isn't evident unless a ship actually enters that bay.

"The bay that opens to the south offers the best means of concealment. Your ships could enter it and stay well concealed. If you make a floating raft disguised as a tiny island, and place the raft at the main entrance to that bay, it will appear as if there is no bay there at all."

Iracema absorbed Siba's idea and then said, "I think what you are suggesting is that Colombo's three ships will enter the main bay and drop anchor. Is that right?"

"Yes, that is correct. And once his ships are at anchor, most or all of his crews would of course desire to avail themselves of the opportunity to swim in the bay and then to go ashore. Once ashore, they would be delighted to meet the inhabitants—us—who await them and invite them to our harvest feast."

Iracema smiled and said, "And then, once Colombo's sailors accept your invitation to join your feast, our sailors would row out past the floating island, into the main bay, and seize Colombo's ships? I like that!"

For the rest of the day, the sailors took groups of local people on a tour of the caravels. Siba asked what the visitors planned to do with the cargo that took more than half the space on board the ships. "I see that the cargo consists of building materials—wood, rope, and other things I have never seen before."

Janaina said, "We have brought enough building material to build one or two more ships such as you see here—caravels. Also, even more pirogues, which are faster to build and sail than caravels. Many of our crew are not only sailors but also experienced ship builders. We are offering to teach your local craftsmen how to build such ships. We had planned on discussing this with you during our presentation, but time got away from us."

Siba smiled. "I for one would be in favor of learning more."

Captain Ruda said, "Perhaps in the morning we can have another meeting to discuss this. For now, our sailors would like to put together a simple structure on land where we can sleep tonight."

During the meal the next morning, the discussion centered on why the visitors had traveled to the island six years before a possible visit by Colombo's ships. Captain Ruda addressed Siba's comment to get the discussion started. "Captain Janaina briefly summarized the future history of the Europeans' exploitation of our world six years from now. Of course, that history may not come to pass, especially given the Malian Federation's successes so far in preventing the

Spanish and Portuguese from leaving their harbors. But we have to be prepared for all possibilities.

"We in the Quonambec communities are hoping to provide the same type of defense that the Malian Federation is attempting to provide along the west coasts of Africa and Europe—through regular, extensive patrols by armed caravels and pirogues. In the past 20 years our Malian ships have either captured or destroyed many Portuguese and Spanish ships attempting to leave their harbors."

Janaina added, "If you all approve, and the building materials are unloaded from the caravels, our crewmembers skilled in boat building can begin instructing those of you who wish to learn those skills. Then, once the training and building is well underway . . ." Janaina paused, looked around and continued, "I will sail one of these caravels back to Quonambec to replenish our supplies of building materials so we can build several more ships." She paused again and added, "Of course I will need to take a small crew with me; perhaps I will find volunteers from among you! It would be wise if the volunteers could learn more of the local language spoken in Quonambec. Some of us have begun instructing those of you who have shown an interest in the similarity to your language. Some may also wish to learn some of the Malian language."

CHAPTER FOURTEEN

The Year 1488

The longshoremen and other workers in Quonambec's main harbor were astonished to see Captain Janaina's caravel drop anchor at the main pier. But even more astonished were the sailors aboard her ship—all 11 of them were indigenous men and women from Guanahani Island. Janaina had recruited people with extensive sailing experience: Isamu, Jun, Humiya, Siba, Bana, Ahiahude, Guabasa, Hiriko, Nanichi, Jin and Guaitiao. The Guanahanians were astonished to see dozens of indigenous, Malian and mixed-race people working at the port. Janaina was also astonished at the number of caravels at anchor outside the harbor. She turned to Siba and said, "There must be 20 ships here! When our little fleet of three ships departed, there were barely half as many ships. It would seem our shipbuilders have been busy. Either that or these ships have sailed over from Cabo Verde or Mali itself."

It didn't take long for Janaina and her crew to disembark. Once they were all ashore Janaina pointed to one of the caravels and said to Siba, "That's the ship Kassa. Its captain is Kareem ibn Hameed." As she was speaking, a group of sailors approached. "Welcome, Captain Janaina! And welcome, brethren from Guanahani Island!" The speaker was an indigenous man; his two companions were Malian. They offered to escort the Guanahanians to the shipping office

"There you can settle into comfortable chairs while a member of the staff will seek out Captain Kareem."

Jin said to Guaitiao, "I can't wait to find out more about this community! Mali and Quonambec… what an alliance."

Guaitiao turned to Janaina. "I wonder if we would be able to have another caravel join us on our return to Guanahani. And with Malian and indigenous sailors!"

"That's a good idea; I'd been thinking of making that request, especially seeing all these ships at anchor. But before making such a request, we have a lot of reporting to do to Captain Kareem and the Council itself."

When Janaina and her crew entered the shipping office they seated themselves around a big table. It wasn't long before Kareem entered from a side door. "Janaina, I didn't expect to see you so soon!"

"What do you mean, so soon? I've been away for two years!" Turning to her crewmates, she said, "Captain Kareem, these are my crew, Isamu, Jun, Humiya, Siba, Bana, Ahiahude, Guabasa, Hiriko, Nanichi, Jin and Guaitiao." Turning to her crew she said, "This is Captain Kareem, formerly of Mali, now working full time as a ship captain in the Malian-Quonambec Federation." She turned back to Kareem. "Captain, I have prepared a full report of our progress on the island and the nearby islands. When this crew and I left to sail here, the people of Guanahani had completed two pirogues and had almost completed their first caravel. That shipbuilding progress was in tandem with voyages to nearby islands to enlist their cooperation in defense against any possible invasion by ships from Europe, especially from Admiral Colombo. The people have also completed many new and improved buildings on Guanahani, but away from the main east-facing bay. They won't be visible to Colombo, assuming his fleet manages to escape the blockade on Spain imposed by our Federal Navy.

"Our specific goal at this time is to ask for your support. Captain Iracema and I, as well as the other captains and community leaders at

Guanahani have estimated we need more building material—enough to build at least two more caravels. And also, many more weapons, including small arms as well as cannons. On top of that we need a supply of long iron bars and rods, nails, and sheets. There doesn't seem to be any iron on those islands."

Kareem smiled. "That's all? I would expect you to ask for much more." He laughed at the reaction from Janaina's crew. "Seriously, your request will have to be taken up by the Council. But I don't foresee a problem. Of course, it would take some time to gather together a large quantity of milled wood, weapons, sailcloth, and other supplies. Not to mention persuading one of the captains of these caravels you see at anchor to either lend you their ship or accompany you to the islands."

Sofia, who had been standing nearby, said, "Kareem, I have had this idea for some time now, and hearing how enthusiastic Captain Janaina is about the progress at Guanahani, I think I want to act on my idea. I would like to provision my caravel and accompany Janaina's on her return to Guanahani. My tasks here have been completed beyond my dreams, and I feel it is time I took on another task. One particular task I think I could perform would be to teach the Guanahani people some rudimentary Arabic. What do you think?"

Kareem smiled. "I am tempted to say you wish to boast of your proficiency in a language that few, if any, of us in Quonambec are conversant in let alone proficient in. But I know you too well. Your idea is not some boast; nor is it a plan to teach a useless language to people who have never encountered Arabic. I think I know the rest of your plan. Why don't you explain it for us?"

"Certainly. When and if Admiral Colombo and his crew arrive in Guanahani, they will have no way of communicating with the local people. We can assume they will not be familiar with Taino or any other language in the region. But we do know that many of Colombo's crew will have some knowledge of Arabic. The people of

Spain, Portugal and the kingdoms of Italy have had many dealings with the Arabs for hundreds of years. The Arabs have controlled the sea lanes south of Europe from the Great Ocean to Greece. That is the principal reason the Spanish and Portuguese are so desperate to find a western route to India—they cannot sail east without deadly confrontations with the hostile Arabs.

"My sisters and I, growing up along the Gambia River in Africa before we were taken as slaves, learned Arabic as our people had commercial relations with Arab traders traveling down from Mali. You also, Kareem, learned some Arabic growing up in the same region. So, in short, I think Arabic would be useful to the Guanahanians by making it possible to communicate with Colombo and his crew."

Janaina looked puzzled. "But wouldn't Colombo be surprised and suspicious to encounter people who spoke Arabic?"

"Not at all. Remember that the Great Admiral believes he will reach India by sailing west across the Great Ocean. He will know some of India's history, especially the history of Arab merchant mariners having extensive dealings with India. When he reaches Guanahani he will believe it to be part of India.

"So, what do you think? Can you spare me and my caravel? With a full crew, of course. I would also like my First Mate Awolu to join me if he's willing."

Kareem smiled and said, "Of course, my esteemed colleague. You and Awolu are free to staff and provision your ship as you see fit. After all, none of the progress the Mali-Quonambec Federation has enjoyed would have been possible without the arrival of you, your sisters and Master Flamel. You have my blessing!"

CHAPTER FIFTEEN

The Year 1490

Lord Keita was astounded at the progress of development on the Cabo Verde group of islands. Each island featured a small village, piers, a loading dock and several fields of crops. Nicolas Flamel was enjoying his role as tour guide to his old friend. As the afternoon turned into evening, Flamel suggested they go to the dining hall on Santiago Island and continue their talk over a meal.

"Keita, tell me more about developments on Guanahani Island to prepare the local people to meet a possible invasion by Admiral Cristoforo Colombo. A report I received said that Captain Iracema's plans have experienced great success in fostering development on the island."

Keita smiled. "Indeed, they have. The people, with instruction and assistance from the Quonambec expedition, have completed an ambitious program of building homes, shipping infrastructure, fortifications and improved farming techniques. In addition, her crews have shown the people how to build sail-equipped pirogues, using the pirogues on board the caravels as models. Iracema has recruited three crews of indigenous people, and they have begun sailing to the nearby islands to assist those people in developing and fortifying their lands. In fact, by now, those projects must be well underway. There is even an ongoing caravel-building project. That project requires more hardwood than the island can grow, which was the purpose of Captain Janaina's voyage to Quonambec.

"While there she obtained another caravel for the return to Guanahani. Captain Sofia brought her caravel with a full crew to accompany her. Before the captains departed, they loaded their ships with hardwood lumber, iron tools, and other building supplies.

"But that reminds me, Nicolas. You might recall hearing about a group of Guanche people from the Canaries who had been abducted in the past and forced to work on board a Spanish ship. Well, a month ago we received a report that the Guanches overpowered the Spanish officers, threw them overboard, and surrendered the ship to a pursuing Malian Navy ship. The Malians took the Guanches back to the Canaries, Gomera Island in fact. Captain Khalil was intrigued by the report. He believed you might be interested in questioning those people because of your past interest in the Berber people, to whom the Guanches are related. According to the Malian Navy officer who prepared the report, the Guanches are striking in appearance—very tall, reddish-tan skin, blonde hair and light-colored eyes."

Flamel set down his glass and was speechless for a moment. Then he said, "Yes, I would be very interested in meeting them. But the question is how would I get there."

"Well, I suspected you might show some interest, so I am prepared to lend you one of the two caravels that have accompanied mine here. They are stocked with building material and other supplies. We will unload the cargo of one of them here. The other will be continuing on to our community in Quonambec. I will put the empty caravel at your disposal."

"Well, that is a very generous offer! I accept. I was preparing to pay a visit to our colleagues in Quonambec, but meeting those Guanches is an opportunity I cannot miss. I propose, then, that you lend me that caravel and its crew for a voyage to Gomera Island. I would of course need to have all identifying markings removed."

Keita looked puzzled. "But tell me, Nicolas, why go on such a long voyage to a tiny island? Surely there is more to this story than merely a chance to talk to some Guanche people."

Flamel chuckled and with a twinkle in his eye, said, "There is indeed more to the story. I have been hoping for an opportunity such as this to land at my feet. My dear Duke, do you remember any of the stories I related to you when I first arrived?"

Keita scratched his chin and frowned. Then he said, "Frankly, I have had more important things to think about than your stories from many years ago. Don't make me guess, just tell me what's on your mind."

"Here's what's on my mind, then. Surely you have heard of the notorious history of Admiral Cristoforo Colombo. Yes? Good, I see you are nodding your head. Colombo is an experienced navigator and ship captain from Genoa. He has long been trying to get the Spanish monarchs to sponsor a fleet of ships to sail west. The imbecile, like all the imbeciles on that continent, believes that if he sails west for a few weeks across the Great Ocean, he will reach India! Can you believe it??? Those fools have no idea how large our world is, or what lies on the western side of the Great Ocean.

"Of course, we are all hoping that the Malian Navy will continue to successfully block Spanish and Portuguese ships from leaving their ports, and that Colombo will never be able to make his historic voyage of `discovery' and exploitation. But there is no guarantee of our continued success.

"But if his fleet does in fact manage to escape our attempts at bottling up those ships in their harbor, we know from the historical record that his little fleet of three ships will be forced to lay over for a little while on Gomera Island for repairs. That's where I hope to arrange to meet the Great Admiral."

"To meet him? You want to meet him, the notorious butcher of the New World?"

Flamel laughed. "Yes, I do in fact want to meet the `notorious butcher of the New World,' as you so nicely described him! Here's why. My plan would be to have my caravel tied up at the dock on Gomera Island when Colombo's ships arrive. I would already have recruited 15 or 20 crewmembers made up of Guanche people to replace the Malian crewmembers, who will journey to one of the other Canaries to assist in development projects there. I would introduce myself to the Great Admiral as a navigator from Paris and explain that I had planned to cross the Great Ocean in search of trade with India. I would tell him that I was hesitant to make that voyage alone; that I would prefer to sail in the company of other ships. I don't believe Colombo would object. I'm fairly certain that Colombo would welcome another ship's company on that voyage, especially a ship captained by a light-skinned man from Paris and a light-skinned, blue-eyed, blonde crew."

"But I still don't understand why you would want to accompany Colombo's fleet."

"Let me explain in more detail. Captain Janaina's report, which you and I have studied, describes her plan. A few days before Colombo's fleet's arrival, she and Captains Iracema and Sofia plan to hide the six caravels and pirogues in the southernmost of the two bays that face the Great Ocean. Janaina says that bay is perfectly shaped to allow that. It has a sharp turn to the left as you enter it, making it possible to hide their ships from view. She plans to place a floating barrier, a raft made to look like a small island covered with brush, across the mouth of that bay in order to discourage Colombo's ships from attempting to enter that bay. Instead, his ships will enter the northernmost bay that opens out onto the Great Ocean.

"Once those ships are inside, the captains anticipate that Colombo's crews would disembark and begin exploring the island and meeting the indigenous people. The people would invite the crews to a feast in the large meeting house far from the beach. All 90 Guanahani sailors would be armed and waiting in the hidden bay in pirogues and other small craft. They will move the raft aside and row out from their hiding place. Some of them will climb Colombo's ships' rope ladders and take possession of the ships. The others will pull their boats up onto the beach, ready to meet Colombo and his sailors when they return from the feast. Of course, Iracema, Janaina and Sofia had no way of knowing my plan. My ship full of Guanche sailors will wait outside the entrance to both bays until they determine that the Spaniards have left their ships. My crew will assist in subduing Colombo's men."

Flamel paused for a few moments to allow his friend to digest what he had just heard. Then Keita said, "I seem to remember you telling me in the past that Colombo had a crew of over 80 seamen. Are you suggesting those men will simply surrender without a fight?"

Flamel laughed. "I am indeed suggesting that! They will have left their ships unattended while they are attempting to ingratiate themselves with the local people. They will be confronted by dozens of armed sailors. Her report doesn't go any further than that."

The Year 1492
August 6

Captain Khalil was frustrated that the little fleet of three ships had escaped his caravel, the Aissata. First Mate Abadir reported, "Captain, we believe that our attack damaged one of the ships before it escaped. The rudder at least was damaged; the ship seemed to be unable to steer straight."

"So, in your estimation, should we resume our pursuit?"

"We could, but I doubt we would make headway. The ships were too far away when we saw them. It was midnight with no moon when those ships left the mouth of the Rio Tinto and entered the open sea."

Khalil was silent for a moment, then said, "If, as I suspect, those ships are the Niña, Pinta and Santa Maria, under the command of Admiral Colombo, then I know exactly where they are bound. In the history Master Flamel studied, the three ships made for Gran Canaria to replace a damaged rudder. From there, according to that history, all three of Colombo's ships rendezvoused a few weeks later at another island in the Canaries, La Gomera. There, they changed their sails from lateen to standard square sails. They then reprovisioned before sailing on a few days later."

Abadir was thoughtful. "Then what, Captain? Do you think we should attempt to confront them there?"

"No, if we encounter them in the Gomera harbor, they will outnumber us and put up a dangerous fight. Plus, we will not have the advantage of surprise. I believe we should follow Flamel's strategy. Flamel will meet Colombo there and introduce his crew of Guanche people. Flamel would ask to follow Colombo's ships as they continue onward across the Great Ocean.

"Why would Colombo agree to have a stranger's ship and crew join his own fleet?"

"Flamel will tell Colombo he is preparing for a voyage across the Great Ocean to open trading contacts with India. India! That fool Colombo actually believes he is on a voyage to India. Colombo will welcome another ship in the fleet, for protection. So, when Colombo's three ships reach Guanahani, Flamel's caravel will be following. Someone will be waiting for them at Guanahani Island!"

Abadir laughed, "Ah, yes. I do recall that discussion. A large colony of our people has settled on Guanahani to get ready for the arrival of the Great Admiral! I wish we could be there to join the festivities!"

"Hah, festivities! Hardly. The plan of the Guanahanis is fraught with risk, although it might succeed if Flamel's plan succeeds.

"As the Guanahanis confront Colombo's men, Flamel's ship will block Colombo's ships from leaving the bay. Then his crew of armed

Guanche sailors will row their pirogues into the bay and lend support to the Guanahanis."

La Gomera

Admiral Colombo was perplexed and suspicious. Three weeks before, after his carpenter, Antonio de Cuellar, had replaced the damaged rudder on the carrack "Santa Maria," the flagship of his little fleet, Colombo confronted the owner of the ship, Juan de la Cosa, and accused him of sabotage. "Lord de la Cosa, I am fed up with your attempts to subvert our mission! It was you who weakened the rudder so that it would crack and fail. Admit it!"

De la Cosa puffed out his chest and grew red in the face. "May I remind you that this is my ship and it was commissioned by the Queen Herself to lead your foolhardy expedition. Why would I sabotage my own ship?"

"Your cowardice is the reason. You never wanted to agree to the Queen's request. You hoped a broken rudder would keep your precious ship within the safety of the Rio Tinto's banks. Instead, it broke after we were well away from land. In addition, we were attacked by the cursed Portuguese and almost lost your precious ship as well as the crew!"

"You have no proof of what you claim."

Colombo knew that de la Cosa was right; the rudder could well have been damaged during the assault by the Portuguese ship. But nevertheless, at Colombo's insistence, de la Cosa agreed to disembark at La Gomera Island. After he had retrieved his ship's trunk, he turned to Colombo and said, "I shall leave you and your mongrel crews at the mercy of sea monsters and storms. I shall seek reimbursement from the Queen should my beloved Santa Maria fail to return to Spain."

After that confrontation with de la Cosa, Colombo experienced a most intriguing event as his ships were being provisioned for the journey to India. While examining the various bills for purchases, he was approached by a man who spoke French and said he was from Paris. That was startling enough—a Frenchman named Nicolas Flamel many hundreds of miles from his home. But his story and his crew were even more startling.

Seeing the skeptical look on Colombo's face, Flamel said, "Admiral, I can see by your expression you doubt my story. I wish I could assure you of the truth of what I am saying."

"Well, you can start by telling me why and when you left Paris. Oh, and your crew; here I see some 15 Guanche men on your ship, a very stout caravel with no markings at all." Colombo smiled, pointed to a nearby tavern and said, "At least let us be comfortable while you spin your tale."

The tavern was an airy, clean room with high ceilings, large windows, half a dozen large tables, and very decent ale. Once they had sat down and ordered food and ale, Flamel began his story. "I have not been a mariner for very long, Admiral. In fact, until a year ago, I was living a very comfortable life as court astrologer and physician to Princess Anne of France, the older sister of Charles VIII. She acted as regent for Charles until he would come of age. Unfortunately for me, Charles did not like me at all; hated me, in fact. I constantly feared my life would be in danger once Charles became king. So, I convinced Anne to sponsor a trading voyage to India. She provided me with funds and two caravels. I have only been on this island for a few weeks. Not being an experienced mariner, I was frightfully sick for most of the voyage."

Colombo set down his ale, wiped his mouth, and laughed. "That is a very amusing tale, Master Flamel. And one I'm not sure I believe. But I do know a bit about the French Court, and am familiar with stories of that family. I am more curious about your crew; or I should say, your French crew. Where are they?"

Flamel adopted a pensive expression. "They left me, Admiral. Said I was crazy to even consider a voyage across the Great Ocean. They took possession of my other caravel and said they were returning to France. So here I am, preparing for a voyage into the unknown with a crew of local men who assure me they are experienced sailors."

Colombo sat back in his chair and studied Flamel. "Now, please tell me why you want to embark on a voyage across the Great Ocean. And what cargo will you be carrying?"

"Quite honestly, what choice do I have but to continue west to India? I cannot return to France, or indeed to most of the other lands bordering France. At least not yet. I still have my ship full of cargo— manufactured goods, for the most part—that I hope to trade for spices, silks and other exotic commodities. I hope to be able to return, at least to Genoa if not France, in a few years. Perhaps Charles will have no influence there."

"Genoa! That blessed land is where I was born." Colombo pushed away his plate and glass. "I will allow you to follow my little fleet. Let us go to my beloved Santa Maria. I will introduce you to my crew. In a few days we should be ready to depart. Will you be ready by then?"

"I hope to be ready by then. I am relieved that you will allow me to accompany your fleet. I look forward to the voyage."

Nicolas was relieved that Colombo kept the introductions brief; he merely told his crew there would be an additional ship joining the fleet. Afterward, Flamel returned to his caravel and brought his crew up to date. His first mate, Ayoze, reiterated that he and the rest of the men were eager to exact some vengeance on the hated Spanish. He said, "This will be repayment for several years of Spanish attacks on our homeland." Flamel repeated what he believed would occur once Colombo's ships entered the bay at Guanahani Island. His crew was eager to get under way.

September 6—A five-week voyage begins

Colombo was neither pleased with the weather nor the lack of progress across the Great Ocean. He muttered to himself as he gave the wheel to his first mate and walked to his cabin. "Four weeks of squalls alternating with burning sun. Much of the food is spoiled! And if that isn't bad enough, my crew are complaining like children."

But he was soon to find out it was worse than children's complaints he would hear. His Master-at-Arms, Diego de Araña, and his boatswain, Bartolome Garcia, approached him the next morning. "Captain, the crews on all three ships are demanding we turn around and return. What shall we tell them?"

Colombo was tempted to threaten to keel haul any sailor who said that to him to his face. But he decided to compromise. "I would like you to announce to the men that I have every confidence we will soon sight land. Remind them of the sea birds we have seen in the last few days. If we do not sight land in the next few days, I will order the fleet to turn around and return home."

That seemed to calm most of the men somewhat. But their calmness was soon a thing of the past. Their food was full of maggots, except for the ship's biscuit, which was hard as a rock and had to be dipped into the foul drinking water before it could be eaten. Several times their ships were becalmed beneath the blazing sun. A few times whales seemingly tried to overturn their ships. Colombo was nearly ready to declare the trip a failure and order the ships to turn back to Spain.

October 1—Getting ready for visitors

Iracema, Janaina, Sofia, Siba and Guaitiao went carefully over the list of tasks that had to be completed before the projected arrival of

Colombo's ships. Iracema asked, "Siba, have the people inspected the floating raft blocking the entrance to the southern bay?"

"Yes, they have. And I have personally climbed on it and made sure it was not in danger of sinking. I also made sure the caravels, pirogues and the smaller craft were securely tied and out of sight of the mouth of the bay."

Sofia said, "The large dining hall has been expanded to accommodate an additional 80 or 85 men. Our own people will number over 100. The food and drink will be more than adequate. I have tasted the beer the local people have made and I must say the alcohol content is quite high. I would imagine Colombo and his men will be quite intoxicated by the time they stagger back to the bay. That will be when the real party begins!"

Janaina asked, "What about the language barrier? How many of your Arabic students feel comfortable with the language?"

"Oh, they're quite good. At least a dozen of them will be the official greeters when the Spanish set foot on shore. The Spanish, believing they have arrived in India, might try to speak to them in one of the Indian languages. Then they will try Arabic. They will assume that those who don't speak Arabic had not had much contact with Arab merchant seamen."

October 12—Arrival!

It was decided. Colombo realized that if he and his crew were not to starve or become seriously ill because of the bad food and water, they would have to turn around. But before he issued that order, miraculously, land was spotted. Shouting erupted among the crews. "India! It must be! We are saved!" Those were the most common shouts of his men. But Colombo, although relieved at the sight of land and the prospect of fresh water and food, was none too sure the land they saw was India.

With his megaphone Colombo shouted his order to enter the bay straight ahead. The entrance to the bay was large. The bay was long and opened out to the right. Colombo saw that the water was clear and appeared to be uniformly deep. He saw no reefs or islands in the bay. Relieved, he ordered the men to drop anchor. He turned to his first mate and said, "I think we shall swim to the shore. The water is calm and I am sure it will be warm in this heat. We could use a bath, and so could our clothes, God knows!"

The mate gave the order—"All sailors in the water. Keep your clothes on. Now! Assemble on the beach."

It took several minutes for everyone to jump off the ships. It took them even longer to enjoy the warm water before swimming to the beach.

Once they were all standing on the beach and gazing at the beautiful greenery all around, they noticed several dozen people approaching. Colombo ordered his men to stand where they were. He told his interpreter, Luis de Torres, to stand by him and wait for the local people to come closer. "I want you to greet them, tell them we come in peace and in search of trade. Tell them we come from Spain. And smile! I see that none of them appear to be armed, so I believe we will not be attacked."

"Captain, what language shall I speak? The only languages of India I know are Hindi and Punjabi."

"If these people don't understand you when you speak to them in those languages, speak Arabic. I believe many of the people of India possess some knowledge of that heathen language."

When the local people were close enough, de Torres spoke to them in Hindi first, then Punjabi. The response of the people was blank stares. But when de Torres tried Arabic, there were smiles and responses. Siba spoke first, "Greetings and welcome to our land. Where have you come from?"

De Torres said, "We are from Spain, here on a trading mission ordered by our monarchs, King Ferdinand and Queen Isabela."

Siba turned to her companions, said something in a language de Torres did not know, then turned back to him. "We do not know that country or your monarchs. But no matter. We look forward to trading with you. But first, won't you join us for our harvest feast? We have a large dining hall that I believe can accommodate you and your crew. Will you come?"

De Torres translated the invitation for Colombo, who told him to ask whether they should change into dry clothes. De Torres said to Siba, "We accept your most gracious offer. We are wet. Shall we go back aboard our ships to change into dry clothes?"

Siba said, "That won't be necessary. In this heat, you will be dry before we reach the dining hall. It is behind those fields and trees. Come! Let us eat and drink!" She turned and signaled for the other Guanahanians to begin walking slowly back to the dining hall. The Spanish, relieved at the amount of trust the people displayed, followed in anticipation of a good meal and fruitful trade negotiations.

When Iracema saw the last of Colombo's crew disappear into the fields, she gave the signal for two dozen swimmers to remove the floating island, exit the small bay and climb the rope ladders on the three ships. Once the swimmers had done that, she ordered the remaining 66 sailors from the Malian caravels to row out of the bay in the pirogues and other boats and pull them up onto the beach. All the sailors were armed. They fanned out across the beach so as to block any of Colombo's men from reaching the water. There they waited.

The dining hall was full of tantalizing aromas of roasted meats and maize. Local people were lined along the sides of the room smiling and holding baskets of flowers. Colombo said to his men, "I have a good feeling about this! I am looking forward to a good meal and some profitable negotiations." His men obviously felt the same to judge from the looks on their faces.

Two older local men stepped forward and said in halting Arabic, "Welcome to our mid-day harvest feast. Won't you please be our guests; there is plenty of food and drink." He stepped aside and motioned for the sailors to take seats at the tables.

As only a few of the local people spoke Arabic, and even fewer of Colombo's crew spoke it, there was little conversation. But that suited the sailors, who were famished and exhausted. The feast went ahead with great gaiety, eating and drinking.

Finally, Colombo arose shakily from his seat, looked around at the people in the hall, and said in Spanish, with de Torres interpreting, "Good people of India, God has indeed blessed us all in this most fortuitous meeting. Our journey across the sea was long and arduous, but at last we arrived at our destination. We look forward to sitting down with you again tomorrow to discuss our trading interests. But for now, I believe my crew and I need to go back aboard our ships to sleep." With that, he signaled to his men to arise. Then he bowed to his hosts, turned and began walking toward the doors. His men followed.

The walk back to the beach seemed to be longer and more difficult than the walk from the beach. Often men would stumble and fall. Several were unable to get back up without assistance.

Finally, they emerged from the fields, but stopped short in amazement when they saw what awaited them as they stood on the beach. A long line of men stretched along the beach at water's edge. Colombo said to his first mate, "I don't understand, and I don't like the look of this. What's going on? There must be more than 50 men lined up in front of us."

His mate looked out past the line of men and gasped. "Captain, look at our ships; they have been boarded and lamps have been lit. There must ten or more men on each ship!" Then the mate turned around and looked behind them. "Oh no! Captain, behind us our hosts have formed a line to equal the one in front of us."

Colombo didn't hesitate, but perhaps he should have. He shouted, "Charge forward, men! Attack!" The `charge,' as it were, was more like a comedy. The weaponless men lunged, but then most of them fell on the soft sand. Colombo saw it was hopeless to continue charging forward, so he shouted, "Turn around! Run back to the field!" That was an even harder command for the men to obey. Those who managed to stand, turn around and commence running, were met with a few dozen smiling villagers. Smiling, but holding wooden staves.

Once Colombo saw that the situation was beyond hopeless, he shouted, "Stop. Everyone, stop!" Mr. de Torres, understanding his captain to be surrendering, shouted in Arabic, "We surrender. We have no weapons." The men stopped and dropped to their knees, hands in the air. Some appeared to pass out; whether from shock or from inebriation, Colombo couldn't say.

A dozen villagers, staves in hand, walked cautiously forward. At the same time, all of the sailors along the shore behind the Spaniards walked forward, weapons in hand. Hiriko shouted, "You will not be harmed if you do as we say. Lie face down with your hands behind your backs." The Spaniards complied. Colombo looked up as his hands were being tied and saw Sofia. He muttered in astonishment, "An African! An African woman!"

Sofia walked over to him and said to him in Portuguese, "Ah, the famous Admiral Cristoforo Colombo, of whom I have heard so much. I am very, very pleased to meet you. More so, under these circumstances." She burst out laughing.

Colombo grumbled, "Stop speaking that cursed language!" Then he lowered his head back to the ground.

Sofia laughed again. "Excuse me for offending your honor, Admiral. I would have addressed you in your native language, Genovese, if I could."

Then she heard shouts from her sailors. "A ship! A ship! A Malian ship is entering the bay!"

She turned toward the entrance to the bay and saw a caravel hoisting a Quonambec flag moving slowly into the bay. As it drew closer, she squinted at it and then shouted. "Flamel. Master Flamel, on one of our ships!"

But what surprised her even more than seeing her old friend on a caravel was seeing what looked like a dozen tall, fair-skinned men crewing the ship. As the ship dropped anchor, several of the sailors lowered two pirogues. Flamel and two of the sailors climbed down the rope ladder into one of them, and three more sailors climbed down into the other. When the two pirogues reached the beach, the sailors got out and pushed them out of the water and onto the sand. Flamel stretched and shouted, "Oh, it feels so good to be on solid ground and off that cursed ocean!"

Sofia walked up, smiled and shook his hand. "Greetings, Nicolas! You arrived just in time. Actually, you arrived after the party is over. You would have enjoyed it."

"Well, I tried my best, but I didn't want to spoil the surprise. I have quite a tale to report to you, but it can wait. Would you like my men to help you find suitable accommodations for these poor, miserable sailors? Oh, before I forget, allow me to introduce these five— First Mate Ayoze, and sailors Derque, Beneharo, Aythami and Afche. They are Guanche men, part of the crew I recruited on one of the Canary Islands."

At that point, Siba and Hiriko walked up and introduced themselves in Arabic. Siba said, "We have heard so much about you, Master Flamel. How do you like the welcome we have given to these poor, miserable sailors, as you so aptly described them?"

Everyone laughed. Flamel said, "I apologize for my poor Arabic." Then he scratched his head as he gazed across the sand at the supine prisoners and said, "I do wonder how the sailors ended up like this."

Hiriko said, "We treated them to a grand feast with plenty of food and drink. Are we to blame if they drank too much and began running this way and that?"

Colombo raised his head and stared at Flamel. He said in French, "You, Flamel! What's going on here? Do you know these people? If so, order them to release me and my men!"

Flamel smiled. "I'm afraid I do not know them; except for this beautiful African lady here. Allow me to introduce you. This is Captain Sofia Amina of the Quonambec-Mali Federation; formerly of Oporto and before that, the headwaters of the Gambia River." Then he said to Sofia in French, "This angry and somewhat inebriated sailor is Admiral Cristoforo Colombo, sailing under the flag of Spain. The rest of these sailors on the ground are his crew." Before Sofia could respond, Nicolas looked around and continued, "My goodness! Whatever happened to them?"

Sofia sighed. "My French is poor, I'm afraid. My Portuguese is much better. May I answer you in Portuguese?"

Colombo interrupted with a shout, "Speak French!"

Sofia laughed and said to Flamel, "Okay. We prepared a party for 80 after we learned they were probably going to arrive today. Luckily, we had just enough food and beer on hand. But our guests drank too much and proved to be somewhat rude. They refused to acknowledge our hospitality. They insisted on trying to reboard their ships, those that you see in the bay, but were too drunk. My sailors kept them from charging into the water in that state, for fear they would drown."

Colombo shouted, "Liar! This is a trap, although I do not know why. Let us end this. Release me and my men."

Nicolas said, "You are right, Admiral. This trap was prepared for you. I am afraid I deceived you back in the Canaries. You are now guests of the Quonambec-Mali Federation. You will not be mistreated unless you refuse to cooperate."

"Cooperate? Guests? Is this how you treat guests, tying their hands behind their backs face down in the dirt? Explain yourself!"

"Well, you and your rulers, Ferdinand and Isabela, would have planned to exploit and enslave the peoples of the New World once they learned it was not India. Myself, Captain Sofia, and all the other people you see on this shore, were prepared for your arrival and were determined to put a stop to the aggressions of the Spanish and Portuguese. Consider yourself our guests. As I said, you will not be mistreated if you cooperate."

The first order of business was to decide what to do with the Admiral and his crew. For the rest of the afternoon and evening, they were separated from one another. The Guanche sailors moved them to several warehouses used for storing agricultural produce and dried fish. Ayoze, Flamel's first mate, spoke fluent Spanish and explained the situation to Colombo and his men. "We cannot release you yet. As a group, you are dangerous. Singly, or in twos or threes, perhaps you would be safe to release. But not here; not on this island. It is already overpopulated and lacks sufficient resources for you."

Colombo frowned. "What do you mean resources? Why don't you return us to our ships? We will return without troubling you further."

"I'm afraid we cannot do that. We know your history well. We intend to change that history. Master Flamel will explain everything in the morning. For the rest of the evening, get some rest."

October 13—Time to unpack

Iracema had studied Colombo's muster roll and learned that there were several carpenters and surgeons on the list. There were also many former farmers. All were healthy, strong, sailors. She turned to Janaina. "I suggest we retain the surgeons and carpenters and transport everyone else to the other inhabited islands nearby."

Janaina looked up from her review of the names and professions listed on the muster roll. "Yes, there are many small islands within two day's sail from here. I remember them as appearing fertile and inhabited. They probably have small populations of Taino-speaking people. I would guess there are many subsistence farmers on those islands. Perhaps these Spanish farmers would be able to help the local people improve their farming methods. And since the Spanish sailors did some fishing during their voyage here, they would have ample opportunity to do that on those islands."

"I agree. And the first task is to teach Colombo and his men the Taino language, or at least give them some conversational ability. We also must urge the local people on those islands to take in some of these Spanish farmers." Then she chuckled and said, "Who knows, perhaps the Spaniards and the local people will become friendly!"

Flamel and Ayoze visited the three warehouses and explained what Colombo's sailors could expect over the next two weeks. "Two of the local people, Siba and Hiriko, are organizing a Taino language immersion course for you. Every day, for five or six hours, you will learn some of the language. Your meals will be brought to you."

The Spaniards protested. They saw no reason why they would have to learn a 'heathen' language. Colombo said, "Explain yourselves. What are your plans for us?"

Flamel smiled. "Once your language course is completed, we will transport small groups of you to the various, beautiful islands near here. You will be introduced to the local people, who will help you adjust to your new life. Perhaps you will find wives among the local people. Cheer up! It could have been worse."

Colombo was not the only one asking detailed questions and protesting. Flamel and Ayoze explained that there were more than 20 inhabited islands scattered around that region, and each of them had fertile land for farming, small inlets for fishing and friendly people eager to help and be helped.

While that was going on, the sailors from Flamel's, Janaina's, Sofia's and Iracema's ships began examining the cargo on Colombo's three ships. On the flagship Santa Maria, which was a huge carrack, they found much that would be useful to the farmers on the islands—great quantities of fabrics, finished clothing, cotton, wool, tools, rope, glassware, and lumber in various lengths and widths. The other two Spanish ships were stuffed with similar cargo. It was decided to use the Santa Maria, Niña and Pinta, as well as four of the local caravels, to distribute those supplies among the inhabited nearby islands, and drop off the Spaniards along with the supplies.

Flamel called a meeting with his Guanche crew. "Soon those ships will depart with these Spaniards. At that point, you and I have a choice. We can either return to the Canaries, or we can proceed on a year-long voyage to Quonambec itself."

A lengthy discussion ensued. Most of the men seemed eager to travel to a new land and experience Quonambec. Flamel said, "If you decide on that voyage, you will need to learn a little Arabic. I will ask one of the local people here who have learned the language to join us. Siba, for example, has an excellent knowledge of the language, and she visited Quonambec once before with Janaina's crew." Several of the men who did not want to proceed to Quonambec voted to remain with the Guanahanians to assist with relocating the Spaniards.

CHAPTER SIXTEEN

The Year 1495

Iracema's caravel glided smoothly into the main Quonambec harbor and dropped anchor. It was late afternoon, and she could see other ships tied up at the piers being unloaded of their cargo. Her crew, made up entirely of Guanahanians, were eager to get onto solid land and walk around after a year on the ship. She said, "Don't go far. I still have to arrange to have the cargo offloaded. That won't take long and then we can wander around and take a look at the progress they've made here."

After she hired the local men and women dock workers to off load and store the cargo, Iracema and her crew began walking around the busy port. She was surprised to see three Federation ships showing some apparent damage from cannon fire. Just then a sailor from one of them came down the gangplank and greeted her. She returned the greeting and asked, "What happened to your ships?"

His expression was a mixture of relief and sadness. "Well, what happened to us wasn't half as bad as what happened to our enemies."

"Your enemies? Where?"

"We were flying Spanish flags and patrolling near the Portuguese port in the fog when we were surprised to see a group of Portuguese ships not far behind us. They immediately began firing at us. Each of our ships was hit several times, but thankfully above the water line. In the end we managed to sink our attackers. Luckily none of the damage to our ships was significant."

Iracema asked, "What did you do after the attack?"

"We decided to sail out to our base in Madeira and report that somehow our patrols off the coast of the Iberian Peninsula failed to stop those Portuguese ships. Our base commander decided to organize a large fleet to sail back to the Peninsula and stage a series of attacks on Portugal, disguised as Spanish ships.

"After making our report, we made some repairs and sailed west across the Great Ocean. We arrived several days ago. It's been over a year since we were attacked. I wonder how much damage our Madeira fleet managed to inflict on Portugal."

"Quite a bit. Overwhelming, in fact!" Abadir came walking up, grinning, and clapped Iracema on the back. "Captain Khalil and I were taking on supplies at our Madeira base when the Madeiran fleet returned. Their fleet commander reported that every section of the Portuguese port was utterly destroyed, along with at least a dozen ships. When the Madeiran fleet left, all that was left of the port was on fire. The commander laughed and said he would have loved to see how the Portuguese reacted to the attack by a `Spanish' fleet."

Iracema smiled and said, "That is indeed good news! Let's hope for a massive retaliation.

"Now, I have some good news for you, unless you've heard it already. Three years ago, the Spanish Admiral Cristoforo Colombo and his fleet were captured at the island of Guanahani."

"Yes, I did hear that. About a year ago, when Captain Khalil and I returned here after our tour patrolling the Iberian coasts, we saw one of Colombo's ships tied up at these docks. The crew on that ship, a huge carrack that Colombo had named the `Santa Maria,' told us the story of Colombo's arrival in Guanahani."

Iracema said, "It was quite dramatic. Literally dramatic. We staged a feast for him and his crew, got them drunk, and took them prisoner. We had been waiting for them, you see, thanks to Nicolas

Flamel's 'advance' knowledge of history. Eventually, we managed to train the Spaniards in the Taino language and distribute them throughout the islands near Guanahani. That carrack you mentioned is one of Colombo's ships. We 'borrowed' it to use a cargo vessel. He won't miss it!"

Abadir laughed. "Good old Master Flamel! Speaking of Flamel, we just missed seeing him. When we arrived, we learned that he and his crew of Guanche men had been here for almost a year before departing for Mali. Do you know what his plans were?"

Iracema frowned. "When he was with us, his immediate plan was just to sail from Guanahani to Quonambec with a crew of Guanche sailors. He hadn't said anything to me about his plans after that."

"Well, from what I've heard about the hatred the Guanche have for the Spanish, I wouldn't be surprised if they're hoping for revenge of some sort."

The Year 1497
January—Niumi, Mali

"You look well, Khadijah. And how is Hassan?" Nicolas was sitting across from Khadijah in the parlor of her house in a well-to-do section of Niumi.

"He is doing well. All that sea air. He now works as one of the harbor masters. No more sailing for him."

Flamel nodded. "I certainly understand that. The same is true for me. My last adventure with the Guanche men turned out very well. I thought that after I brought them here to Niumi for the final campaign against the Spanish, I would do something different."

He decided to change the subject. He stood and looked out the window. "You have a beautiful view of the harbor. Do you remember the first time we came here?"

Khadijah groaned. "Yes, all too well. My sisters and I were riding horses and boats through savannah and jungle with Duke Keita." She stood and joined him at the window. "You know, Keita was a great leader and a good man. I miss him."

"We all miss him. He and I were good friends all these years."

Khadijah smiled and sat back down. "And just how many years has it been since you showed up in Mali, my friend?"

Flamel groaned. "Normally, I don't like to talk about my age. People look at me and tell me I don't look my age when I tell them I am 78."

"But dear Nicolas, you lie to them. It has been 79 years since you turned 78 back in Paris. It was that infernal spherical astrolabe that did this to you, wasn't it?"

Nicolas gazed out the window before turning back and looking directly at Khadijah. "Yes, I believe so. I suspected it would happen as I was making the alterations to that infernal machine, as you call it."

"You mean it would stop your aging process?"

"Yes; the machine stopped me from aging. Or, I should, say, it kept my body from aging. My mind keeps telling me I'm 159 years old. When will it stop, I often wonder?"

Khadijah paused for a few moments, then said, "I have an idea, but you might not like it."

"An idea? About what?"

"An idea for allowing yourself to age. That is, if you want to age. Some people don't want to age. They don't like the idea of getting old. How about you? Do you want to resume the aging process?"

Now it was Flamel's turn to pause. He looked around at Khadijah's beautifully appointed living room, then turned back to her. "I think I know what you're thinking. It's my amulet. I began wearing it after my first trip to the distant past. You remember when I told you I had acquired this from the treasury of Emperor Charlemagne in the year 1,000? It originally belonged to the 9th century Caliph Harun al-Rashid of Palestine. I wore it when I travelled to Hawaii in the distant future. That was when I realized the power of the astrolabe had been absorbed into the amulet. Not needing to be carrying around a bulky astrolabe, I deposited it in Hawaii. That was where Horacio Fuente found it not long afterwards."

Khadijah sat silent, recalling the occasion when Nicolas told her that. Then she got up from the divan and joined him at the window. Without turning around, she said, "Nicolas, why not give it up? You've accomplished your goals, haven't you?"

"I believe I have. But I am nervous about what will happen to me, to my body, to my mind, after I take this amulet off."

"Well, allow me to suggest that you wait not much longer. Long enough to find out whether our Malian Navy has been successful in its next, and biggest, campaign against Spain."

Flamel could see by the expression on Khadijah's face that she was worried. He walked over to her and hugged her. "I learned yesterday that your daughters and nephews will take part in that expedition. What are your thoughts?"

"My thoughts are that there will be casualties in that naval attack on the Spanish port, and some of those casualties will be Malian. I fear that the attack will not be as simple as the one I took part in 37 years ago, burning shipping docks and a handful of caravels. No, Nicolas, this expedition has a greatly expanded goal—the complete destruction of the Spanish port of Huelga and all of the ships. There will be fighting, I am sure of it."

"Khadijah, I wish I could assure you that our forces will be victorious and the power of Spain will be destroyed, utterly destroyed forever. Just like we destroyed the power of Portugal two years ago. But, of course, nobody can predict the future." Then he laughed.

"Your laughter reassures me, Nicolas. Do you know something that none of the rest of us know?"

"Nothing is certain, my dear. But my vision of the future we are creating reassures me. But let us change the subject. What of your niece, Aliyah, Maryam and Yousef's granddaughter? What news do you hear of her?"

"It has been a few years since she last paid me a visit. She wrote recently to tell me she is very busy in her internship with the Quonambec City government. She's only 16, Nicolas, and I worry she will decide on a career in the navy, like everyone else in the family."

"Well, I can certainly understand your worry. I have no children myself, but still, I worry about the dangers all these young people face today."

"Nicolas, thank you for your concern. Now, about your visit here—what are your plans? Are you going off on a new adventure?"

"No, I am going to remain here in beautiful Niumi. No plans other than that. Except to remove this beautiful amulet that has served me so well. But I won't remove it quite yet. I want to wait for news of a successful campaign against Spain. And also, I want to work on a project I have in mind."

He paused and added, "That reminds me, when last I and the Guanche sailors were with Sofia in Guanahani, she had organized a plan to 'distribute,' so to speak, Colombo and his sailors all around the islands in that area. Have you heard any news about her and that plan? After the Guanche men and I left Guanahani, we spent a year in Quonambec before sailing here. The men wanted to come here to join the campaign against Spain."

"As a matter of fact, I have, Nicolas. Her distribution plan was wildly successful. So successful in fact that several of the Spanish sailors that she 'transplanted' to the other islands married local Taino women. The Spanish sailors with specific skills needed in Guanahani remained there. The report said those Spaniards were happy there."

She turned and walked over to the divan and sat down. "What's the project you're working on, if I may be so bold?"

Flamel walked to the door, retrieved his satchel, walked back to the divan and sat beside Khadijah. Opening the satchel, he pulled out a sheaf of papers. "Here, take a look and tell me what you see."

Khadijah took the sheaf from Flamel and looked at the papers. "This is written in Portuguese." She turned back to Flamel and said, "Nicolas, it's been many years since I've spoken Portuguese, 61 years, in fact. I was a slave in Oporto for five years, which is when I learned Portuguese. The duke who had 'bought' me in Africa—not far from here in fact—loaned me to a priest when he returned to Oporto. Thanks to Father Martim Rodrigo, I and my sisters repaired the spherical astrolabe you modified and came here to carry out your plan. Do these papers tell that story?"

"Only part of the story, my part and those parts played by people I interviewed. I am asking you to supplement the story with the part you, your sisters and Father Rodrigo played."

Khadijah smiled. "And the part Gabriel Hugo played."

Flamel raised his eyebrows. "Ah yes, of course, my young apprentice back in Paris."

"Well, he was no longer young when Father Rodrigo asked him to repair the astrolabe. Quite ancient, in fact."

June—Huelga, Spain

The Castillian princes were losing the battle, and they knew it. By Admiral Alonso Fernandes' count, his fleet had lost 10 ships. But he dared not order the ships under his command to turn and flee, let alone surrender. He turned to his subordinate, Lieutenant Rodrigues, and ordered him to signal the remaining 20 ships in the fleet to sail straight at the imposing Portuguese fleet and fire every weapon they had. "But Admiral, that is suicide. There are over 40 Portuguese ships, and they are all around us. They trapped us into leaving the harbor to engage them. You yourself estimated there were only six or seven ships firing at our port buildings, as they have done many times before."

"Did you not understand my order, lieutenant? Issue the command, or I will have you shot and thrown overboard!"

As the admiral turned and walked away, Lieutenant Rodrigues did something he never thought he would have to do in his long years in the Spanish Navy—he violated a direct order. Instead of signaling as the admiral ordered, he signaled a general retreat. After a few minutes, when he could see the rest of the Spanish fleet turning away from the battle, he shouted, "Admiral Fernandes, our ships are fleeing! Your direct order that I relayed, they have disobeyed!"

At first, the admiral was tempted to countermand the order himself. But then he realized that if he did nothing, he would not be blamed for the action of the rest of the fleet. "Lieutenant, we have no choice. We cannot fight the Portuguese alone. Turn around! Let us leave the battle before we are destroyed."

However, leaving the battle was impossible. As his lieutenant had observed, the Spanish ships were surrounded by Portuguese ships bent on destruction. As the day wore on, more and more of the Spanish ships could be seen burning and sinking. Finally, Admiral Fernandes ordered his ship to surrender. Up went the white flag. After a few more minutes, there came a signal from the closest Portuguese ship, still some distance away, that the sailors aboard Fernandes's ship must lower their boats, board them and row away from the caravel. The Portuguese would then fire on the caravel and sink it.

Once Fernandes's crew had done that, they watched as their ship was bombarded with fire pots and cannon fire. It caught fire and eventually sank. Then, to his crew's surprise, the Portuguese ship turned and sailed back toward the port. Once the remnants of the other burning Spanish ships in the bay were sinking, the rest of the Portuguese fleet sailed back to the port. Soon, Admiral Fernandes could see that fleet begin firing on the port buildings and ships again.

And again, and again. For the next two hours, as the light of day faded, it was replaced by the light of burning buildings.

CHAPTER SEVENTEEN

The Year 1506

Aliyah, a young woman on holiday from Quonambec, had come to visit her elderly great aunt Khadijah at her home in Niumi, the capital of Mali. To her surprise and sadness, the ancient housekeeper, Nicolas Flamel, informed her that Khadijah had passed away two nights ago in her sleep. The housekeeper handed Aliyah a book handwritten in Portuguese and said, "Your great aunt, with my collaboration, wrote it in a language most people don't understand these days. Your dear Khadijah wanted you to keep it safe and in the family. She intended to give it to you last year, but you were unable to pay her a visit then."

She held the book in her hands and paged through it, marveling at the beautiful handwriting and binding. It was bound in black leather with chain stitching. Embossed on the leather cover was the title: <u>Um Tempo Longe do Tempo</u>

But she was puzzled at why Khadijah would write the book in Portuguese. In Aliyah's youth, she had studied Portuguese at the insistence of great aunts Khadijah and Sofia, and her grandmother Maryam. She recalled an occasion when she was dining with her grandparents and great aunts. They were explaining why she should study Portuguese. She had complained, "But why Portuguese? That little country in Europe is a poverty-stricken backwater; nobody goes there." She turned to her grandfather, Hassan. "You agree with me, don't you?"

"Actually, I agree with my beautiful and headstrong wife. Although I was forced to learn the language of the hated Portuguese during the year when I was a slave on a Portuguese sailing ship, I soon came to value the language. Now, of course, very few people speak it. But there is a vast literature written in Portuguese, including historical accounts of the days when Portugal dreamt of creating its plan of world domination. That plan, thanks be to God, never came to pass." Hassan paused and smiled. "The plan failed because of the wars between Portugal and Spain. The two would-be rivals for world domination through slavery and colonization repeatedly attacked one another's ships." When he said that, he chuckled and said something that Aliyah found puzzling. "Ah, I remember those battles well. Such strategy your grandmother and her sisters devised!"

Sofia frowned at Hassan. "Dear Hassan. We mustn't spoil the surprise. Let Aliyah learn the truth of those battles when she reads the book." Then she said to Aliyah, "Please, even if you never have to use the language it's important that you know our history." Then she smiled and said, "You will learn the origin of those wars!" After she said that, she chuckled and repeated, "I think you will find Khadijah's book extremely entertaining and enlightening."

Now, years later, after not only Khadijah's passing but Sofia and Maryam's as well, Aliyah had some free time on her hands. The last of "The Three Sisters," as they liked to refer to themselves, had passed away. So… she opened the book and began reading.

ABOUT THE AUTHOR

After 23 years practicing law with the California Attorney General's Office in San Francisco, and teaching for 13 years in Golden Gate's Appellate Advocacy program part time as an adjunct professor, I retired in 2011 and began writing fiction and memoirs. My first opus was a novella, *My Brother's Keeper*, loosely based on the circumstances of my younger brother's murder. Next came a novel, *Stolen Identity*, published in 2015, and its sequel, *Unfinished Business*, in 2017. My short story, *One More Race Before We Die*, was published in 2019 in the University of Hawaii eZine, *Vice-Versa*. After that story was published, my novel, *The Mystic and the Warrior*, came out in 2021. The novel *Around the Horn and Back* came out in 2020. *Trial and Error*, the third novel in the trilogy that began with *Stolen Identity* came out in 2021. My novel, *The Spherical Astrolabe*, came out in 2021. I published a collection of stories in *Collected Stories* in 2021.

I published three memoirs in 2021: *A Pirate Forever*, *From Librarian to Lawyer*, *Life as a Peace Corps Volunteer Ethiopia and Eritrea, 1972-74*, and *The Happy Wanderer*. While still a law student at Golden Gate, I served on the Law Review and published an article, *Qualified Immunity for INS Church-Busters? Presbyterian Church (U.S.A.) v. United States, Golden Gate University Law Review, Ninth Circuit Survey, Volume 20, Number 1, Spring 1990*. In the year 2000, I published a memoir of my Peace Corps experience in Asmara, Eritrea, in the *Peace Corps Writers* anthology, *Eritrea Remembered: Recollections and Photos by Peace Corps Volunteers*.

SELECTED WORK by
MICHAEL BANISTER
(in chronological order)

My Brother's Keeper

A drug courier crashes his plane in a frozen lake in Yosemite's high country. Winston, a Yosemite "valley rat" on the run from killers in his home town, discovers the plane during a winter hike. He off loads the cargo and begins a new life as a drug dealer. After he and his girlfriend are murdered during a drug deal gone south, their two unrelated children, Josh and Kathy, are raised by their respective grandparents. When Josh asks his Uncle Mark for help in finding his "sister," the outcome is anything but predictable.

Stolen Identity

Dushan's dreams had always been unusual—sometimes scary, sometimes exhilarating. But ever since he was seven years old his dreams took on another dimension—it was like he was awake inside them. His mother—who he thought had been killed in the Yugoslavian civil war when he was a baby—was talking to him, telling him she was alive and living with his father—who was supposed to have been lost at sea during a fishing expedition in the North Sea. In each of those dreams, Dushan was unable to respond and tell his parents that he was living with his "adopted" family in California and was best friends with his "stepbrother" Danilo. The two stepbrothers were now teenagers and occasionally popped up in one another's dreams, sharing their impressions after waking up. However, the time for dreaming was past—they were about to embark on a desperate attempt to escape their abusive father, the man who arranged to steal Dushan from his real father and plant the lie that his real parents were dead. Their attempt succeeded on one level, but the consequences were completely unexpected.

Unfinished Business

The exciting sequel to "Stolen Identity," the story of a stolen boy and his beloved "stepbrother" growing into manhood and bringing their two families together. Now, they discover they have some unfinished business to take care of and some very unpleasant people to deal with. This gripping tale follows these young men and their families through Britain, Ireland and Slovenia as they attempt to put an end to the tragedies that brought them all together in the first place.

Trial and Error

Dushan Sava was in trouble. Accused of stealing the identity of the victim of a horrific traffic accident, and then impersonating him as a college student, Dushan, an illegal immigrant, had to flee the country using the victim's passport. A year later, after having obtained his own passport and returned to the US, he accompanied a friend who would soon join the faculty at Rutgers University. Dushan's former roommate saw him on campus, and Dushan was arrested and put on trial. The outcome of the trial was anything but certain.

The Mystic and the Warrior

Who was the man who called himself Shamsuddin? In post-war Valletta, on the island of Malta, he lived in a part of the city that still hadn't recovered from the destruction of World War Two. In 1955, Shamsuddin lived in a bombed-out post office and sold antiques and other valuable items. When a group of five young men from Istanbul paid a visit looking for such things they had heard Shamsuddin could sell them, the parting gifts he provided them were much more than gifts—the young men soon discovered they couldn't bear to be without them.

Forty years later, Shamsuddin's business had radically changed. He had allied himself with Turgut Evren, a Colonel in the Turkish military. Each man had a hidden agenda—hidden from society and hidden from each other. And the five men who were no longer young? What was their destiny in this evolving story?

The Spherical Astrolabe

A group of retired professors from University of Hawaii discover a spherical astrolabe in an attic of a 19th century mansion on Molokai. It had been converted from a device for maritime navigation into a device for navigation through time. Accompanying the astrolabe was a 500-year-old book describing how the astrolabe was converted and what the result was. The professors decided to acquire more of the astrolabes, convert them per the book's instructions, and attempt to travel back to 15th century Mogadishu, Somalia. Trouble was, Chinese Admiral Xheng He's "Treasure Fleet" was in port, and several of the sailors decided to attempt to kidnap the professors and put them to work on the ships.

Around the Horn and Back

What would you do with your dad's broken time machine, a modified "spherical astrolabe?" You could fix it if you had 21st century tools, but you're both in the 15th century. You could pretend it's a normal nautical device and offer it to the 15th century explorer Vasco da Gama. But what if the Great Admiral discovers the true function of the device? How will you edit your dad's memoir to describe the astrolabe as nothing more than an ancient marine navigation device? Will your dad's wannabe time-traveling companions find the astrolabe in the future?

Life as a Peace Corps Volunteer Ethiopia and Eritrea, 1972-74
A collection of aerogrammes, memoirs and photos from my two years as a Peace Corps Volunteer in Ethiopia and Eritrea, 1972-74.

A Pirate Forever!
A memoir of my life growing up in Japan, Austria, Germany and California.

The Happy Wanderer
A collection of memoirs of my travel and work, 1974-2021, in Seattle, Tunisia, Berkeley, Turkey, Oakland and Ireland.

Collected Stories

Four stories:

One More Race Before We Die—Three race car drivers killed in a race ask a Las Vegas magician to stage a race to allow the dead drivers to finish the race.

Gino di Lampedusa—A genie on the lam from an evil genie in his own world passes through the veil and asks a Las Vegas magician to help him capture and neutralize the evil genie.

Whitethorn, 1969—a backwoods commune terrorizes a group of back-to-the-land hippies.

My Brother's Keeper—a loosely based story based on the murder of the author's drug-dealing brother.